"You might be able to hide your feelings from others, but not from me," Sal said.

He looked at Olivia and added, "Your expression gives you away every time."

When she started to put her hands to her cheeks, he stopped her. "Don't try to hide. Not from me."

Deliberately, Olivia backed away from him and the touch that could still turn her inside out.

She knew she was putting off the inevitable, and she hated the fact that she felt cowardly for doing so. She'd never been one to shirk from her responsibility, but now...now she didn't know where her duty lay.

Sal took her hand and squeezed it. "Right now, we're operating in the dark. We don't know who's doing this. We don't know what they want. We need something, anything, to give us a handle on this."

"Okay," she said reluctantly.

"You're doing the right thing."

Was she? She didn't know.

Olivia looked up at Sal, not surprised to find his eyes flat and dark. He was all Delta at the moment.

Good. She had a feeling she was going to need his special set of skills and training.

Jane M. Choate dreamed of writing from the time she was a small child when she entertained friends with outlandish stories complete with happily-ever-after endings. Writing for Love Inspired Suspense is a dream come true. Jane is the proud mother of five children, grandmother to seven grandchildren and the staff to one cat who believes she is of royal descent.

Books by Jane M. Choate

Love Inspired Suspense

Keeping Watch
The Littlest Witness
Shattered Secrets

SHATTERED SECRETS

JANE M. CHOATE

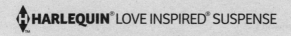

LOVE INSPIRED BOOKS

ISBN-13: 978-0-373-45709-0

Shattered Secrets

Copyright © 2017 by Jane M. Choate

www.Harlequin.com

Printed in U.S.A.

For thou, Lord, art good, and ready to forgive; and plenteous in mercy and to all them that call upon thee.
—*Psalms* 86:5

To Dina Davis, editor, whose suggestions for this book
made it much richer and stronger.
To my friends at Front Range Christian Fiction Writers.
Thank you for all the encouragement and support.

ONE

A hiss of energy brushed her face as the deadly blade cleaved the air a scant inch from her cheek.

Olivia Hammond forced herself to remain still. To move even a fraction would cause the knife to slice open her skin. She dared not breathe until the need for oxygen forced her to take a noisy gulp of air.

"Ah, I see I have your attention. Now you will tell us where you hid it. Maybe we will kill you quickly rather than taking our time about it." The heavily accented voice held no particular menace, as though the man who pressed the weapon to her face was discussing a business transaction rather than taking her life.

"Or we will be forced to *encourage* you to tell us." This was from the second man who had said little during the interrogation.

The two intruders had already ransacked the law offices of Chantry & Hammond. It had been her misfortune to return for a file and run into them.

"I don't know what you're talking about." How many times had she uttered those words? The effort of not moving and the fear of what the men intended to do to her had dulled her energy and her wits.

Don't give up. The small voice inside her head had her sitting up straighter despite the duct tape binding her to the chair. She was far from beaten. Her passion for defending the underdog had earned her a reputation for taking no prisoners, both in and out of the courtroom. She called upon that now.

It was up to her to free herself. No one was coming to her aid. Immediately her mind rejected that. There was always One who was at her side.

Lord, I'm in a fix here. I need Your help. The silent prayer said, she tried once again to reason with her captors. "Why don't you tell me what it is you're looking for?"

"Enough!" Impatience shimmered in the single word. The first man, whom she'd identified as the leader, nicked the delicate skin of her cheek with the blade.

Blood trickled down her cheek. The metallic scent of it stung her nostrils and sickened her stomach.

"You know what we want. Do not play the innocent. You are part of this, along with your boss, trying to cheat us out of what is ours."

"Calvin?" What did this have to do with Calvin Chantry, the head of the law firm where she was an associate? And where *was* Calvin anyway? He hadn't shown up for work yesterday or today.

"Yes. Calvin. Your boss. He could not pull this off without help. You, his partner's daughter, are the logical choice."

Though the man spoke English, she struggled to understand his thick accent that gave a hard jab to every syllable. "Please… Calvin didn't tell me anything. I don't—"

A key turned at the office door. Teresa, the cleaning lady.

Olivia held on to a breath of hope. Just as quickly, the sliver of hope died. Teresa, sixtyish and stout, would be no match for two armed men.

An exclamation in the woman's native Portuguese was quickly followed by the clump of her sturdy shoes down the carpeted hallway outside the office. Seconds later, a fire alarm shrilled. Teresa must have pulled it.

Thousands of gallons of water spilled from the sprinkler system above.

"This is not over," the first man said just before he and his partner fled.

Drenched, Olivia waited for help and said another silent prayer, this one in gratitude for the Lord's intervention.

An hour later, after the fire department had arrived and departed and the EMTs had checked her over, she was still answering questions from the Savannah police, some in uniform, some in plain clothes. She didn't fool herself that *she* was that important. The Chantry & Hammond law firm, a Savannah institution, carried a lot of weight.

"I don't know what they were looking for," she repeated. "They kept saying I knew where *it* was. And then they accused me of being in on it with Calvin Chantry."

"Did the men say what it was they wanted from Chantry?"

"Like I said, no."

Olivia shivered in her wet clothes. "If you don't mind, I'd like to go home and change."

The older of the detectives, whose suit bore the stains of a quickly eaten dinner, nodded. "Sure." He handed her a card. "If you think of something, anything at all, give us a call."

After promising to do so, Olivia headed home. Though a long shower helped to rid her skin of the memory of the knife and the stench of her own fear, she admitted what she hadn't wanted to just an hour earlier: she needed help.

She picked up the phone and punched in the number of the man she had thought never to see again. She needed the kind of help that only Salvatore Santonni could give.

At core, Salvatore Santonni was still a soldier. He shoved a hand through his hair. Though he'd left Delta several years back, he had only recently exchanged the military haircut for a nonregulation one. He missed the buzz cut that had been his for more than a decade.

Now an operative for S&J Security/Protection, he took the jobs assigned him with the same dedication to duty with which he had carried out missions for his country. Individuals contacted S&J only when circumstances had turned dangerous and they needed a bodyguard.

When he'd gotten Olivia's call, he'd driven through the night, unable to wait until morning. He knew she wouldn't have called unless she was terrified. He rapped on the door of the Savannah law offices of Chantry & Hammond.

Olivia Hammond let him in and stared up at him, her mouth forming a soft O, her eyes widening. He took a moment to take inventory of her. Tall and willowy, she was elegant in a red suit. He imagined she thought the severe style made her look powerful, even tough, in the courtroom where she shredded witness testimony on a regular basis. Instead, it only emphasized the delicate femininity that was so much a part of her.

Sun-streaked blond hair swung to her shoulders, framing a face that was so breathtakingly beautiful that he couldn't look away even if he wanted to. Which he didn't. Her features weren't perfect: her nose was slightly too small, her lips too full, but together, they made for an arresting package.

Something flitted through her eyes, but he couldn't make out what it was. His eyes narrowed when his gaze zeroed in on the bandage that marred the perfection of her cheek. He fisted his hands at his sides to keep from reaching out and skimming his fingers over it.

"It's nothing. Only a prick of a knife," she said softly.

His hands tightened at the thought of men threatening Olivia, using a knife on her. Even though he'd decided that he and she couldn't be together, he cared about her. Always would.

"Olivia." Just her name. It was all he could manage. The feel of it on his tongue was infinitely sweet.

She looked down, away, and then gestured to her office. "Let's talk inside."

He followed her into the office. His tongue seemed stuck to the roof of his mouth so he looked about. Water damage from the sprinklers was as evident here as it was throughout the suite of offices.

Even with the damage, though, he could make out the spartan decor. A desk with an efficient-looking chair behind it, a couple of battered file cabinets and two uncomfortable chairs for visitors comprised its only furnishings. He remembered her saying that comfortable chairs invited visitors to linger and she had too much work to do to indulge in small talk.

"Thank you for coming. I didn't know who else to call. I know Shelley would have come, but she's like a hundred months pregnant."

Sal smiled at the exaggeration. Shelley was eight months pregnant and counting, but to hear her tell it, Olivia's description was more accurate.

Olivia looked down at her hands. "You didn't have to come, but I'm glad you did."

He schooled his voice to a coolness he was far from feeling. "You called. I came." Because he cared about her. Whatever had transpired between them didn't change that. "You had to know I would."

"I wasn't sure." The silence stretched until the air was thick with it. "I figured you never wanted to see me again." A punch of hard silence followed.

He ignored the past and focused on what was important. "What's going on, Olivia?"

"I told you over the phone. Two men broke into the office. If it hadn't been for Teresa—the cleaning lady—

they'd have killed me." She recited the words by rote, probably having said the same thing to the police.

"Can you describe them?"

She gave a detailed description that had him nodding in approval.

"What about their clothes?" he asked.

"Their pants dragged on the floor. One man kept having to yank his up. He looked annoyed each time he did it and I remember wondering why he just didn't wear clothes that fit."

"Prison shuffles," Sal said, naming the pants in question. "Anything distinctive about their voices?"

"They both had an accent, but I couldn't place it. It wasn't Spanish. I would have recognized that."

"Middle Eastern?"

"More guttural." She shook her head. "I don't know. I was too busy concentrating on not throwing up on their shoes and making them really angry at me." The last was said with a half smile that quickly died.

Sal kept his voice quiet as he asked further questions. The last thing Olivia needed was for him to come on like gangbusters. She looked fragile enough to break. Who could blame her? Being held captive and threatened with torture and death was enough to send anyone into a tailspin.

She picked up a mug of coffee from her desk, her hand trembling so much that she had to set it back down again. The small gesture was telling in the extreme, but he pretended not to notice. Just as he pretended not to notice that his own breathing was having a tendency to stutter.

"What did they want?"

"I don't know." Her already husky voice turned even huskier.

"You said the men mentioned your boss. Where is he?"

"I haven't seen or heard from him in two days."

"I don't believe in coincidences," he said, thinking aloud. "First your boss disappears, then you're threatened by two men you've never seen before. The two have to be connected."

"I don't see how. Calvin would never have anything to do with men like that."

"He's a lawyer. Lawyers work with all kinds of people, including 'men like that.'"

There was a new edge to his voice now, and he worked to gentle it. Olivia wasn't one of the men he'd commanded in his unit. She didn't snap to attention when he barked out an order.

In an attempt to curb his impatience, he lifted his gaze to study the vivid print hanging on the far wall. Fortunately, it had escaped being drenched with water. Bold colors depicted a boat docked at the Savannah harbor at sunrise, the clashing tones juxtaposed against the quiet scene. That was Olivia, he thought, both bold and quiet.

She was a contradiction in many ways. Right now, she was frightened and looking to him for help, both in keeping her safe and in finding out what the men were after.

"I'm here now. You're not alone."

And with that, tears gathered in her eyes.

"Ah, Livvie." The nickname came automatically to his lips. He watched—oddly helpless—as she swiped at the tears now trickling down her cheeks.

He had fast-roped from a helicopter into choppy seas, done HALO drops from 30,000 feet, and escaped the clutches of a warlord who'd put a price on his head and a target on his back, but he was as clueless as the next man as to how to handle a woman's tears. Helpless wasn't an emotion that sat well on his shoulders.

Being with Olivia had always been emotion-laden and fraught with unspoken feelings and unanswered questions. Those too-short weeks with her had been the best of his life. She'd filled him, and all of those dark places inside of him had grown a little smaller, a little brighter. He couldn't forget that, didn't want to forget it, even when he'd realized there was no hope for a future between them.

Though he'd fallen in love with Olivia, he knew he wasn't the right man for her. The violence in his past made him unworthy of her. He'd walked away from her two years ago, certain it had been the right choice. The only choice. So why was he regretting it now?

After spending most of the night answering the police's questions followed by a full day in court, Olivia returned to her office, slipped off her jacket and toed off her shoes, yawning heavily. She'd worn a lipstick-red suit, a favorite that gave her much-needed confidence. She had splurged on it last year, living on macaroni and cheese for the following month in order to afford it, and wore it on days like today when she needed a boost.

Feminine vanity had her wishing she didn't look as exhausted as she felt, and she put a hand to her hair to push it back from her forehead. Out of habit, she sat behind her desk while Sal took one of the uncomfortable chairs in front of it.

"Why?" The question had taunted her all day. "Why did those men come after me? I don't know anything." The breath tumbled from her lips at the memory of the wicked-looking knife pressed to her cheek.

"Someone thinks you do," Sal pointed out.

"Not helping." She tried a smile, but it came out flat.

"Sorry. It's likely you know more than you think you do. A couple years ago, you were Chantry's right hand. I'm guessing that's still true."

"I suppose. But that doesn't mean I know what those men were talking about." A fresh shudder poured through her.

Across the desk, Sal reached for her hand, squeezed. She glanced at him, then away.

Two years ago, he'd overwhelmed her with the strength of his personality. She felt a frown take hold before she could stop it. That had been part of the problem, her fear that he would consume her, that her own sense of self would be eroded if she stayed within his orbit. Not even the most expensive of suits could help with that.

Had she done the right thing in calling Sal for help? She knew of his work for S&J Security/Protection, knew he would protect her with his own life, but could she afford what that protection involved? Inviting him back into her life spelled trouble, if not disaster.

He'd broken her heart when he walked away. If it happened again, she wasn't sure she'd survive.

"This case you're trying, is there anything about it to make someone threaten you?" he asked, breaking into her thoughts. The pensive quality in his voice told her he was trying to make sense of the attack, just as she was. The knowledge that he was on her side warmed her.

"You mean aside from the millions of dollars it's going to cost the company if we win?"

"Yeah. Besides that."

Deep lines scoured Sal's forehead. Despite that, he was more attractive than ever. His appeal came from something that went much deeper than superficial good looks to the very core of the man. The steadiness in his gaze, the acceptance of who and what he was, would always set him apart from other men. There'd been a time when her heart had raced when she looked at him.

His large body blocked much of the light given from the desk lamp, but even in that muted light, she could detect the near black of his irises. They were a compelling color. Just like the man himself.

"I'm looking for something more personal. Anything that would give someone a score to settle with you."

"I'm the lawyer of record. Another member of the firm could have handled it, but I wanted it." After twenty-one children had died as a result of the company substituting fake medicine for the real thing, the parents had retained Chantry & Hammond to represent them in the deaths. Her lips drew tight in silent fury at the thought that children had died due to greed.

Olivia pushed her chair back from the desk, stood and started to pace. "Parents are depending upon me to get justice for their children. I have no intention of letting them down." Or herself.

"You care about the kids who died, their parents." The quiet understanding in Sal's voice was balm to her soul.

A few disgruntled colleagues, two in particular, had accused her of wanting a big payoff as her part of the settlement. Olivia hoped the settlement the parents received would be generous, but no amount could make up for the loss of a child. She planned on donating any fee she made to the families, many of whom were still paying off medical bills.

Tears leaked from her eyes over what the parents had endured. No parent should lose a child.

Sal rose, started to move toward her, then paused.

Olivia noticed an odd expression in his eyes and wondered what had caused it.

He didn't give her the opportunity to puzzle over it. "What's Chantry been working on lately?"

The abrupt change of subject startled her, causing her to stop midstride as she thought about it. "He's been spending more and more time away from the office. He told me he's practicing for when he retires." A half smile touched her lips before slipping away. "I teased him that he wouldn't know how to retire. He gave me this funny look and said I might be surprised."

"Funny? How?"

She lifted her shoulders. "I don't know. Just different."

Though Sal seemed disappointed that she couldn't be more specific, he didn't press the issue. "Okay. Let's try another tack. Tell me about him. What he likes. What he doesn't. Who he hangs out with."

"You can't believe Calvin has anything to do with this." She couldn't keep her irritation from showing. He didn't know Calvin the way she did or he wouldn't be asking questions like this.

Tension crackled.

"You said the men mentioned your boss," Sal reminded her.

"So I did, but like I told you, Calvin would never have anything to do with men like that. He's too—" she searched for the right word " refined." Her stomach rumbled, and she flattened a hand against it with an embarrassed laugh. "It's been a long time since lunch."

"Come to think of it, I'm hungry, too. I'll run out and get us something. Is Thai all right? I saw a restaurant advertising genuine Thai cuisine around the corner. We can talk while we eat."

"Perfect."

In truth, she welcomed a few minutes to herself. Sal's presence filled the small office, as though the very air was absorbing his unflagging energy and unflinching courage. She wanted to breathe it in, that potent mix, and take it inside her. At the same time, she felt almost light-headed as the strength of his personality threatened to consume her. And then there were the disturbing questions about Calvin.

She leaned back, closed her eyes and felt some of the strain of the last twenty-four hours leave her body.

It was then that the call came, the call that sent her world into a freefall and her emotions into a frenzy of fear.

"We have your boss." The mechanically altered voice, giving no hint as to who was speaking, sent a chill of foreboding skittering down her spine. "Wait for further instructions. Do not go to the police or FBI, not if you want to get Calvin Chantry back alive." A breath-stealing pause. "If you tell anyone about this, you will both pay the price."

Olivia's thoughts raced, even as her heart did a double beat. The threat was clear: talk and she'd put her life as well as Calvin's in jeopardy.

She wasn't a coward, but right now, she was scared right down to her toes.

TWO

After spending ten years in the mountains of Afghanistan, Sal was still adjusting to being home in Georgia, with its supercharged humidity and honeyed air. Though he'd been back in the States for over three years, he was still struggling with the difference in climate. The heavy smog that had hung over the city was absorbed into the darkening sky and was only a memory, but the humidity hung in the air and played havoc with his right shoulder, which still carried pieces of shrapnel from enemy fire, a souvenir from his days as a sniper's spotter. Even in the air-conditioned offices, he felt the clamminess that clung to his skin like cheap polyester.

But it wasn't the heat or even the energy-stealing humidity that caused him to go on high alert. Something was wrong. His senses flared in alarm at an unknown threat.

He felt it in the tension that pulsed in the air, saw it in the drawn lines that had moved into Olivia's face in the short time he was gone to pick up dinner.

"What is it?"

She turned away for a few seconds as if gathering her thoughts. When she faced him once more, she smiled brightly. No doubt she believed she'd successfully hidden whatever was bothering her, but it wasn't good enough to fool him. "Nothing. Why do you ask?"

On the surface, she sounded calm, even convincing, but something was off. Her smile was too wide, her voice too determinedly cheerful. Her eyes were full of turmoil that hadn't been there thirty minutes ago. She'd barely picked at the plate of steaming food he'd set in front of her.

"Something happened. You might as well tell me because I'm not going anywhere."

"What? Are you my keeper now?" The harsh words appeared to have surprised her as much as they did him.

"Olivia." He kept his voice soft. He didn't want to spook her. "What happened?"

"I'm sorry. I don't know what I was thinking, bringing you all the way here. I realize I overreacted about the whole break-in thing." She gave a forced laugh, the sound only deepening the taut atmosphere that charged the air. "I'm fine. Really." Another laugh. "I appreciate you coming all this way, but you don't need to stay. I'm sure you have real work, something better than babysitting me."

The dismissal in the words had him wincing. Well, she'd find that it wasn't so easy to send him packing.

Sal went at a problem straight-on and didn't turn away until he had a solution. Seeing Olivia again wasn't the usual kind of problem. Charging at it full speed ahead wouldn't change the way things had ended between them. Nor would pretending that he no longer had feelings for her.

Right now, he had to put those feelings away and find out what she was hiding from him. That required finesse, not Delta strong-arm tactics.

"You don't look fine. You look like you'd blow away if I breathed on you too hard." It was no exaggeration. Olivia looked like a strong sigh would topple her. Shadows, as deep as a Georgia night, had taken up residence under her eyes.

Her earlier smile had vanished, a frown taking its place. "Thanks. I needed that." The sarcasm in her words didn't get to him, but the flash of hurt in her eyes did.

Sal wanted to kick himself. From the moment he'd shown up in Olivia's office that morning, he'd blundered. Big-time. The drive from Atlanta to Savannah, plus worry for Olivia, had ratcheted up his impatience and sent his tact, never abundant under the best of circumstances, into a nosedive. That was no excuse, though.

Something had caused Olivia to turn her back on his help.

"You know I can't leave you. Not like this. Tell me."

Her frown darkened into a scowl, the lines of it so hard that he thought her face would break. She squared her shoulders, as though she needed to shore up her resolve. Chin pulled in, she gave the impression of a queen looking down at her subject. The effect was mitigated by the quiver of her lips. "I told you. I'm fine. You can go back to Atlanta."

Sal had been trained in interpreting microexpressions, those unconscious gestures that revealed far more than words. His Delta unit had been assigned to Counter Terrorism for a stint.

The CT boys knew their stuff when it came to ferreting out information from suspected terrorists. Once back in the States, he'd gone to work for S&J Security/Protection, named for its founders Shelley Rabb Judd and her brother Jake Rabb.

Shelley, an ex–Secret Service agent, had shown Sal other tricks in detecting lies. Not much got by him.

Olivia's gaze kept sliding to her left, a telltale sign that she was lying. "You have to go. Please."

The plea in her voice caused him to frown. Gone was the calm of a moment ago. She sounded frantic. He was more certain than ever that something was going on, something that terrified her at least as much as last night's attack.

"What aren't you telling me?"

She shook her head from side to side, as though willing away whatever had scared her. "N-nothing."

Sal fitted his finger beneath her chin, raising it until her gaze was level with his. She held it for a moment before looking away. "You always were a poor liar."

"I'm not lying."

"No? Then why can't you look me in the eye?"

"Please, Sal." Her voice hitched on a tiny sob. "You don't understand."

He placed his hands on her shoulders. "What don't I understand? Tell me, Livvie. I want to help."

"It's Calvin. Someone took him." Her shoulders trembled beneath his hands. "They said if I contact the police or the FBI, they'll kill him." She waited a beat. "And me, if I tell anyone."

Sal took a moment to absorb that. "I'm not police or FBI," he pointed out at last. "What are you going to do?"

She thrust out her chin. "I'll find out what they want and deliver it." The steel was back in her voice.

Sal kept his face impassive, but his mind was churning through possibilities. None of them good. As capable and intelligent as she was, Olivia was no match for kidnappers. He wasn't going anywhere, but first, he had to convince her that she needed him. "What if I promise to not interfere and to keep a low profile?"

"I can't risk it."

"I'm afraid you don't have a choice because I'm not leaving."

"Then I guess you're staying." The begrudging tone told him that she didn't want him there but was glad he was there anyway.

A smile tugged at his lips. That was Olivia. Self-sufficient to a fault. Her mouth trembled, though, mute evidence that she wasn't as confident as she pretended. If he hadn't looked closely, he would have missed it.

Olivia put a hand to her mouth, as though aware of the

giveaway. He didn't comment on it. She wouldn't appreciate the observation.

For a fraction of a moment, he wondered why he was trying so hard to convince her to let him help.

Not for the first time, he wondered why he had been born with a conscience that was as much taskmaster as moral compass. He should walk away from Olivia and her problem, content in the knowledge that he'd tried to help. The few times he'd ever ignored his conscience, however, he'd lived to regret it.

He had enough regrets to last several lifetimes.

One look at Sal and Olivia knew she'd have a fight on her hands to convince him that she could handle this on her own. The sharp angles of his face were cast in even harsher lines than usual.

It was his warrior face, one she'd seen only once before but the memory was forever etched in her mind. Two men had tried to rob her and Sal as they'd left a restaurant one night. One of the men had pushed her to the ground, causing her to cry out.

Sal had taken them down quickly and efficiently. When he'd turned to her, the ferocity in his eyes had sent her pulse into overdrive.

"The police will be here in a minute," she'd said to defuse the anger that radiated from him.

"They wanted more than to rob us. If they had hurt you…"

"I'm okay. Thanks to you." The experience had made her determined to never again be so powerless and she'd started studying martial arts.

He still wore the mantle of the soldier he'd been across his shoulders, telegraphing an innate desire to protect, to defend, to stand between danger and those weaker than himself. He was a good man, an honorable man, whose self-assurance and unshakable sense of justice defined him as much as the dark hair and skin that hinted at his Italian ancestry.

Against her will, Olivia felt herself responding to his appeal. To him. That stunning realization unfolded in the space of one heartbeat and shocked her into stillness. With an effort, she did her best to ignore it.

He looked the same as he had the last time she'd seen him, right down to the off-center dimple that punctuated his chin. She longed to smooth her finger in that shallow dent. Deliberately, she fisted her hands at her sides to keep from doing that very thing.

She couldn't deny the frisson of pleasure she'd experienced when he'd walked into her office that morning as the sky grew pink with dawn. Nor could she shake off the sweet memories that assailed her, memories she'd locked away for two long years.

Olivia wanted to believe he was here because he cared about her, but she knew better. She pushed from her mind the unwelcome memory of how they'd parted, and concentrated on the present.

She let her gaze take in the man who had once meant so much to her. At five feet and nine inches, she was hardly petite. Still, she had to look up at Sal, who stood a good five inches over six feet. Broad shoulders, narrow waist and legs that were as sturdy as telephone poles, not to mention a military bearing, gave him an imposing presence.

No, there was nothing soft about Salvatore Santonni. With hard planes and abrupt angles, his face would never place him in the pretty-boy category. It had too much strength and stubborn resolve for such insipid looks and bore the lines and ruggedness that came from long hours exposed to the wind and the sun. His dark eyes missed nothing and portrayed a startling intensity.

Arms folded across his wide chest, he broadened his

stance as though preparing for resistance. He knew her too well and had already anticipated her response.

But how else could she react? This was Calvin's life they were talking about. She had to do what the kidnappers said. Exhaustion and hunger dragged at her, but it was the riot of emotions roiling through her that had turned her stomach inside out and her mind to mush.

She wet her lips. "I can't risk involving you," she said at last, panic rising with each syllable. "The kidnappers will know."

"How will they know?"

"I don't know." She all but shouted the words. "All I know is that I have to do what they said. If I don't… Calvin will die. I can't let that happen. I won't let it."

"Just how do you plan to get him back? Ask nicely and hope the kidnappers play by the rules?"

Resentment filled her. Sal wasn't responsible for bringing Calvin home safely. She was. With renewed purpose, she squared her shoulders and braced herself for what came next.

"You won't get Chantry back on your own. Take a breath and then we'll decide on our next step."

"You can't be here. They'll know."

Sal knelt in front of her. "You can do this. *We* can do this. But we have to be smarter than the bad guys." He took her hands and folded them inside his own. "Whoever's behind this is counting on you reacting with fear. You're smarter than that."

"Am I?" She hated the self-doubt in her voice and looked down at their clasped hands. Then raised her gaze to his. His dark eyes locked on hers. She saw strength and courage there. Maybe she could draw on some of his when her own was so lacking. Before she thought better of it, she voiced her thoughts aloud.

"I didn't want to call you." The admission cost her,

but she plunged on. "I didn't want to lean on you, but I'm doing exactly that."

"You can lean on me whenever you like," he said.

In that instant, she thought of the Lord and remembered that He'd said that all who came to Him could lean on Him.

She'd never doubted that the Lord would be there for her, but a man she hadn't seen in two years was asking her to put Calvin's life in his hands. Could she do it? Unbidden, the memory of Sal leaving her with scarcely a goodbye intruded into her thoughts, sending a spear of pain through her.

"Lean on you like I did two years ago?" She flushed at her rudeness. Sal had made the trip from Atlanta to Savannah solely to help her. He didn't deserve the back side of her tongue.

His lips thinned, but he didn't respond to the barb.

She wanted to snatch the words back, was about to do just that, when he said, "You have to see that you can't do this on your own. These people don't play fair."

Gone was the apology that hovered on her lips. "I'm not an idiot. I know that."

"I never said you were an idiot," Sal said, his patience underscoring her lack of the same. "You're one of the smartest people I know. But you don't have experience in dealing with this kind of situation."

"And you do?"

"In Afghanistan." Pain darkened his eyes. "A group of insurgents grabbed a couple of locals who had been helping us. They had promised to make an example out of anyone who assisted the US. They had a reputation of being particularly brutal with their captives. My unit was called in to get them out."

The words had a staccato rhythm to them, as though he could pry them out only by infusing every syllable with a mechanical precision. Whatever memory he was recalling obviously wasn't a pleasant one. What he'd left unsaid was somehow worse than what he'd told her. "Let's just say that kidnappings are unpredictable. Things can go south in a hurry." His face morphed into a hard mask, a stark contrast with the gentleness he'd shown her only moments earlier.

Olivia wanted to ask him what had happened, but something held her back. If Sal wanted to share, he would, but she doubted he'd do so.

He had always been protective of her and had never wanted to bring the ugliness of war into her world. It had been one of the problems between them, his reluctance to share all of himself with her.

And what about you? an inner voice chastised. She hadn't shared everything about herself, either. They had each held back parts of themselves, as though afraid they would give away pieces they wouldn't get back should the need arise.

Another regret.

Sal's mind clicked through possible scenarios of Olivia dealing with the kidnappers on her own, each more frightening than the last. She wasn't equipped for it, as he'd tried to tell her.

Judging from her reaction, he'd made his point all too well.

"You're not thinking straight," he said now, his voice gentle. "That's what kidnappers do. They want you off balance so you'll do what they say without thinking it through."

When her phone rang, she jumped. Sal motioned for her to put it on speaker, and she pressed a key. "Yes?"

"You disobeyed instructions." The artificial voice gave no hint as to the caller's identity. Man or woman. Young or old. There was no way of knowing.

"I didn't go to the police," she said quickly.

"But you told someone. Do not bother denying it. Your instructions were to tell no one. Now you will pay the price." An ominous pause followed. "More precisely, Chantry will pay the price."

"Wait! Please wait."

A second voice. "Olivia, please. You have to do just as they say…" Calvin's words ended in a scream.

Sal watched as Olivia held her breath. "Please. Please don't hurt him. I'll do what you want. Anything. Just please don't hurt him again." Her words dwindled to a sob.

"It is too late, lady. Your interference cost your boss much pain."

"It was my fault." She shouted the words in the phone.

"Why didn't you listen? Why—" A hoarse cry followed. And another.

"Calvin!" But Calvin Chantry was no longer on the phone.

"What are you doing to him?" When she swayed, Sal placed his free hand at her waist, steadying her.

"Do you see what your failure to obey the rules has caused? This is on you, Ms. Hammond. Remember this the next time you are tempted to disobey instructions." The voice was all the more chilling for its total lack of expression.

"Please," she cried, voice slurred with shock and grief. "Please stop. I'll do anything. Anything. But please stop hurting him." Tears streamed down her cheeks.

Sal resisted the urge to wipe them away. He understood she wouldn't want his acknowledgment of their existence.

"Then start obeying instructions. Or next time your boss will lose more than a body part." A sly pause. "And you, Ms. Hammond, how would you look without one of your lovely ears?"

THREE

After a night of Calvin's tortured cry echoing in her head, Olivia found herself on her knees, praying for the Lord's guidance. She remained there for long moments, absorbing the quiet of the early morning.

Memories of her boss's screams filled her throat with a lump of fear. She tried to swallow it, but it was like swallowing broken glass. Each shard sliced at her throat, spilling drops of blood and tears.

Why hadn't she followed instructions? Why had she— It was too late for self-recriminations. The only thing she could do was to move forward. And that meant sending Sal away. She couldn't afford to do anything else to antagonize the kidnappers.

Be still and know that I am God. The familiar scripture wrapped its peace around her, and she got to her feet, determined to do what she must.

Sal was a good and honorable man, but she had to keep him out of this from now on. Look what had happened when the kidnappers learned he was helping her. No matter what he said or what experience he'd had in dealing with abductions, he was a threat to Calvin's safe return, which had to be her priority.

When he arrived to pick her up, he took one look at her and shook his head.

"You're doing it again."

"Doing what?"

"Wondering how you're going to convince me to go away and let you handle this on your own."

How did he do that? He'd read her mind as though her thoughts were written across her face in bold strokes.

"Your face gives away your every thought and feeling. So don't bother trying to deny it."

"I know you want to help, but this is Calvin's life we're talking about. If the kidnappers learn that you're still helping me, Calvin will be punished." She let her gaze meet Sal's squarely. "Can you accept the consequences of that? Because I can't."

She watched as his broad shoulders stiffened and his lips pulled into a tight line, the controlled anger locked in his jaw a mute testament to his frustration.

Sal wanted to argue with her, to convince her that he was right—she saw it in his eyes—but he didn't try to. All he said was, "I'm staying. Get used to it."

Determination lit Olivia's eyes. He knew that look. It was her I-can-handle-this-by-myself face. While he respected her independence, he couldn't allow her to be hurt because she was too proud to admit she needed help. He knew he had to tread lightly.

He didn't want to scare her. At the same time he needed to make her realize that kidnappings and ransom drops rarely, if ever, went smoothly. She didn't know what she was getting herself into. He'd do whatever he had to in order to protect her. It was time she accepted that.

Olivia reached for his hand, nails biting into his palm. Visceral shock leached the color from her face until her skin appeared almost translucent.

"I'm sorry, Sal. You came all this way and I barely even thanked you."

"It's all right. But don't try to send me away again. Whether you admit it or not, you need me."

"You're right." She twisted a strand of hair. "That's one thing I resented about you. You're always right."

Had he been right two years ago when he'd walked away from Olivia and what they had together?

At the time, he'd been sure it was the right thing to do. He'd left for a reason. That reason still held. His past was pockmarked with pain and despair. He couldn't inflict that upon someone as full of light and love as Olivia.

He couldn't focus on the past. Not now. They had to find Chantry. Both instinct and experience told him the kidnapping was more than a simple snatch-and-grab for money. If that had been the case, Olivia would have already received a ransom demand. Instead, the kidnappers were toying with her, trying to rattle her into making a mistake.

He had to convince her that she couldn't blindly give in to their demands. He'd keep her safe, whether or not she agreed to it. His sense of duty and honor, drilled into him during his years in Delta, demanded that. Though he'd left the military behind, he hadn't left the essence of it in the mountains of Afghanistan. It was in his blood, his pores, his heart.

He wouldn't have it any other way.

When Olivia and Sal arrived at the office, the receptionist greeted them and pointed to a box. "Ms. Hammond, a package arrived for you."

Before Olivia could take the package, he stopped her. "Let me." He withdrew a pair of thin protective gloves from his pocket and donned them. If there were any fingerprints or DNA on the box, he didn't want to disturb them.

"You think this—" she gestured to the box "—is from the kidnappers?"

"I think there's a strong possibility." He looked about the reception area. So far only the receptionist was here, but other workers would probably soon arrive. "Do you want to take this into your office?" Inside her office with the door locked, Sal didn't let go of the package.

She held out her hands. "I'll do it."

He shook his head. "There could be a bomb inside. Probably not. But we have to have it checked."

Her nod indicated reluctant agreement.

Sal made a call to a friend still in uniform, explained the situation. Within ten minutes, an explosives expert arrived and told them to wait outside. A short time later, the man gave the all clear.

"No bomb. Something else." He pushed aside wrapping paper.

Inside lay a severed finger.

Sal and his friend exchanged a grim look. "I don't know what you're dealing with here, Sal, old buddy," the man said, "but you'd better get some help." With that, he left.

Olivia barely registered the conversation. She could only stare. The gasp that escaped her lips was filled with revulsion. She'd expected something like this, but the reality was worse. A lot worse.

"It's Calvin's."

"You sure?"

She nodded. "I recognize the ring. He bought it a few months back. We had just won a big case and he wanted to celebrate." She frowned. "I remember mentioning that it wasn't his style. Calvin said something about maybe I didn't know everything there is to know about him. Then he laughed and patted my hand." She squeezed her eyes shut against the memory.

Sal studied the box with its grisly contents. "The ruby looks real," he said of the large stone set in the pinky ring.

"Calvin would never have had a fake. Real or nothing, he used to say."

"We don't have a choice anymore," Sal pointed out. "We have to take this to the police. It's evidence of a crime."

Of course he was right. She was an officer of the court. If she didn't turn the finger and ring over to the police, she was guilty of committing a crime. But what of Calvin?

Obviously the kidnappers had eyes on her. What she did now could sign his death warrant, but doing nothing wouldn't bring him back, either. She was caught between two untenable choices. The weight of indecision was crushing.

Calvin's screams remained fresh in her memory. How was she supposed to agree to taking the box to the police when she could still hear his cries in her mind? A hard fist tightened in her belly at the acceptance that she was to blame.

"You're doing it again. Blaming yourself."

How did he know? She feigned ignorance, not wanting to admit that he knew her so well.

"You're blaming yourself for what happened to your boss. Don't fall into that trap. You'll never get free." Sal skimmed a finger along her jaw. "You might be able to hide your feelings from others, but not from me. Your expression gives you away every time."

When she started to put her hands to her cheeks, he stopped her. "Don't try to hide. Not from me."

Deliberately, she backed away from him and the touch that could still turn her inside out.

She knew she was putting off the inevitable, and she hated the fact that she felt cowardly for doing so. She'd never been one to shirk from her responsibility, but now... now she didn't know where her duty lay.

"The sooner the police start processing this, the better." Sal stood, grabbed her hand, squeezed. "Right now, we're operating in the dark. We don't know who's doing this. We don't know what they want. We need something, anything, to give us a handle on this."

She needed the wisdom of Someone wiser than herself. *Lord, please help me make the right decision. I can't afford to make a mistake.*

The silent prayer afforded her a measure of peace.

"Okay," she said, reluctance drawing out the two syllables. "We take this to the police."

"You're doing the right thing."

Was she? She didn't know.

Olivia looked up at Sal, not surprised to find his eyes flat and dark. He was all Delta at the moment. Good. She had a feeling she was going to need his special set of skills and training.

She'd kept track of him during the last two years. Stories of what he'd done in his work for S&J Security/Protection frequently made the Savannah papers. Sal was a hero, though he'd deny it with his last breath.

He'd brought home the courage that had defined him as a Delta, risking his life to safeguard others. It would always be so with this man who put country and honor first. Her heart had filled with pride when she'd read the articles chronicling his bravery and resourcefulness.

On top of that, she was still trying to make sense of the feelings swirling through her system at his nearness, making it difficult to breathe. The slightest touch sent sparks arcing between them. Or had she imagined it?

Her instincts couldn't be trusted at the moment. High stress and emotional upheaval were a potent combination. Mistaking vulnerability for something else could only lead to heartache, and she did her best to set aside the complex feelings the last twenty-four hours had stirred up.

She'd managed to take a few deep breaths; at least, she didn't sound like she was gasping for air any longer. She looked at the man who had burst back into her life, riding to her rescue like the hero he was.

His code of honor was a way of life, dictating how he lived and what he stood for. That's why he was here, to help her, to save Calvin's life and maybe her own. No other reason.

She'd do well to remember that.

FOUR

The trip to the police station was made in near silence. Sal slanted a glance in Olivia's direction. The lines that fanned from her eyes and scoured her forehead were new and emphasized the paleness of her features.

Finding a severed finger in a box was enough to send anyone into shock. Added to that was the threat that the same could happen to her. After the initial fright, she'd handled it with a steely resolve he could only admire, but the experience had taken its toll. The shadows under her eyes had grown darker with every minute.

Olivia needed something—someone—to hold on to. And right now that someone was him. Even though things had ended, he still had feelings for her. Guilt over his past gnawed at him. He couldn't ask someone as full of faith and goodness as Olivia to share that with him. Seeing her beat herself up over what had happened to her boss tore him apart.

He'd do his best by her, if only because he didn't know any other way. Doing his best, giving his best had been drummed into him during his Delta days. Deltas never gave in and never gave up.

Outside the police station, Sal pulled into a parking slot and turned to Olivia. Going with instinct and need, he placed his hands on her shoulders, drew her in.

"I don't know if I can do this," she murmured against his chest. "You heard Calvin. I can't be responsible for them hurting him again. I can still hear his screams in my mind."

He felt the shudder race through her and tightened his grip. "You aren't responsible. For any of it." He waited until she stopped shaking before releasing her. "Going to the police is the right thing."

"If you say so." But her tone lacked conviction.

He wasn't going to convince her, but neither could they keep evidence of a kidnapping from the police.

Olivia was an officer of the court, but she was also a woman made vulnerable by her feelings. He knew how intensely she felt things. Whether fighting for a client or fighting for a friend, she gave her all. In that respect, they were very much alike.

He wanted to reassure her that everything would be all right, but she would see that for the lie it was. The truth was, there was no guarantee that they would get Chantry back alive. The kidnappers had already proved how far they would go to achieve their ends. The only thing he could promise was that he'd give his own life before he allowed anything to happen to her.

Sal took her hand and squeezed. "Remember, you're not alone."

The lack of a ransom demand bothered him. Kidnappers always had an agenda. It was obvious they were trying to rattle Olivia, to frighten her into doing whatever they said when they issued the demand. But why hadn't they done so? It made no sense.

He didn't believe for a moment that the people who had taken Chantry would let the man go once they had what they wanted. If anything, they'd be more likely than ever to kill him, and Olivia as well.

There was something else Sal hadn't told Olivia. They

were into day two of the kidnapping, maybe more seeing as how Chantry had been unreachable two days before that. The second day was a threshold. Any possibility of a positive resolution decreased substantially after that. The situation tended to harden up, the danger to the victim rising dramatically.

Sal hadn't shared his worries with Olivia yet. She needed time to regroup before facing the next hard truths.

The police department wasn't filled with bored cops and surly criminals as television shows depicted. Instead, it looked like any other office made up of professional men and women going about their jobs in a purposeful fashion. The occasional shout or cry didn't cause a dozen guns to be drawn. No, the atmosphere was one of grim purpose, flavored with the smells of old coffee and new sweat.

Sal had been in his fair share of PDs during the last several years of working for S&J. They were much like the military, with a clearly established chain of command and organizational hierarchy.

He steered Olivia to the desk sergeant where they stated their names and business to the efficient-looking woman behind the desk. A raised brow and the order to have a seat was her only response.

When a detective appeared, Olivia and Sal stood, followed him through the bull pen and went inside an office. He closed the door behind them. "Detective Richard Nynan. Now suppose you tell me what this is all about."

Sal opened the box, indicated the finger inside and gave an overview of what had transpired.

"You say this belongs to your boss?" Nynan asked Olivia.

She nodded. "I recognized the ring."

"No chance it could have been removed from your boss's finger and put on—" he gestured to the severed digit "—whoever this belongs to?"

"No. The ring was custom-made for Calvin, I mean, Mr. Chantry, to reach the joint of his finger, just like it does. See how the stone tapers at the top?"

"Okay. That helps." Nynan made notes on a legal pad. "I think I have it all." He fixed his attention on Olivia. "You have no idea what the kidnappers want?"

"As I told you the first six times you asked the question, no, I don't."

"Sorry. Just trying to get things straight in my mind." He put down his pen, scratched behind his ear. "It doesn't fit the pattern of an ordinary kidnapping. Usually, kidnappers make their demands up front. They want their payoff right away, whether it's money or something else." Once again, he looked at Olivia. "This court case you talked about—could the kidnapping have something to do with that?"

"It's possible," she said thoughtfully. "If it goes the way I think it will, the company is going to have to pay out a huge compensation package. Twenty-one families are involved."

"So it's back to money."

Sal had remained silent during the exchange, listening and thinking. He saw where the detective was going with this. "You think the kidnappers are going to barter for Chantry's firm pulling out of the case."

Nynan nodded. "I think it's a strong possibility. As Ms. Hammond said, there's bound to be a big compensation package."

"But even if we did pull out of the case, some other firm would take over," Olivia pointed out. "It doesn't make sense."

They'd been over this again and again but kept circling back to it.

"Why kidnap Chantry?" Nynan asked, more to himself than to Sal and Olivia. "Why him?" A few minutes later,

Nynan stood. "I think I have all that I need for the moment. I'm sorry about your boss," he said to Olivia.

She nodded. "Me, too."

Outside, the Georgia sun beat down on those foolish enough to spend more than a minute under its unrelenting rays. Sal hurried Olivia to his truck, helped her inside, then circled it to slide in on the driver's side. He punched up the AC.

"I hope we did the right thing," she said. "What can the police do that we can't?"

"They have resources we can't hope to match."

Her phone chirped. She switched it to speaker phone. "Yes?"

"You disobeyed orders." A pause gave emphasis to the next words. "Involve the police again and your boss will be returned to you in pieces."

Olivia was barely holding it together.

She knew it. Felt it. First the men in her office threatening her. Then the call about Calvin. The box with his finger. The second call. How much more could she take without falling apart?

In the meantime, she still had a case to try, the most important case of her career. Yes, there'd be some prestige to it. More important, though, was the precedent it would set that no company, however big, could pass off fake medicines for real ones and get away with it.

The parents, she knew, could use the money to pay off astronomical medical bills, but nothing could restore their families, make up for the unthinkable loss they'd endured. No amount could atone for the loss of a child.

"I need to work," she told Sal. Of course, the case needed work. But more than that, she needed the purpose of it, the satisfaction of making a difference. A smile slid over her lips. Her daddy had always said that when you had a problem, take it to the Lord first, then get to work. He had lived that right up until the end.

"Okay. But I'm staying close."

Sal's words reminded her of his innate goodness. He didn't back down from trouble; nor did he turn away from those in need.

Covertly, Olivia studied the man beside her. Two years ago, she'd thought she'd known him, but then he'd walked away, shattering her dreams and her heart. They'd gone their separate ways. Not without regret, at least on her part. Though she'd dated other men since then, none had touched her heart the way Sal had. None had come close to measuring up to him.

Olivia didn't deceive herself—she was risking her heart by asking Sal for help. She had briefly thought of calling Shelley Judd instead but had immediately rejected the idea. Shelley was nearing the last month of pregnancy. No way could Olivia involve her friend in this.

She and Sal had shared something special, or at least she thought they had. Shelley had introduced the two of them on one of Olivia's frequent trips to Atlanta to see her friend.

From that moment on, Olivia had known that this was a man who could become important in her life.

Within a week, they were spending every spare minute together, unwilling to let a moment go by without being close. They were so attuned to each other that they could finish the other's sentences.

When she had returned to Savannah, Sal had followed. It had been a glorious six weeks of heady happiness and foolish dreams. Then, without warning, he told her that things weren't working out and she'd do better to find someone else. She thought she'd moved on until she'd seen him again and knew that she hadn't moved on at all.

"I don't know what I would have done without you these

last two days." The acknowledgment caused her cheeks to redden.

"You would have managed, but I'm glad I was here."

Her stomach did a jittery dance at the warmth of his words. As though aware of her thoughts, he drew her to him and held her. Just held her. Did he know that was what she needed at that precise moment?

And then she remembered her vow to keep him at arm's length. Letting Sal back into her life had been a risk from the beginning. She had to remember why he was here.

Pushing away from him, she gathered strength, but her breathing was ragged. Not from the effort of putting some distance between them but from the knowledge that she needed the distance if she were to maintain her sanity.

Sal had always had that effect on her. It wasn't his size, though that was impressive. It wasn't his unflinching courage that was so much a part of him. It was the overall package, strength tempered by gentleness, honesty and compassion.

She and Sal didn't say much on the way to the office. Once there, she planned to go over depositions while he headed to Calvin's office.

"I want to get a handle on your boss," he said in explanation. "If I learn more about him, maybe I can predict how he'll react to the kidnappers. It might help us down the road."

It made sense. Only a few of the partners and associates had arrived, so she was able to get Sal into Calvin's private office without attracting attention.

Olivia spent the next hour working on witness depositions, preparing motions that would be reviewed by the court and writing a brief. The work was tedious, but it soothed the ragged thoughts that swirled through her mind.

How did the kidnappers know what she was doing practically before she did? How had they known she'd called

Sal? How did they know she and Sal had gone to the police? She trusted the employees of Chantry & Hammond implicitly and couldn't imagine any of them kidnapping Calvin, but that didn't answer the question.

In many ways, the law firm was her family. When her father and Calvin had started it decades ago, they'd built more than a business. They'd forged a family of friends. How could she suspect anyone who worked there of spying on her, of abducting Calvin?

She'd lost her father five years ago to a blood clot that had moved from his leg to his heart with frightening speed. It had been Calvin who had stood beside her at her father's graveside and held her as she wept. She'd turned to him with work and personal problems, depending on his experience and pragmatic nature.

How would she survive if something happened to him? She had to get him back. She *had* to.

The prayer that sprang to her lips came without thought. Taking her problems to the Lord was second nature, had been since the time she'd been a small child, frightened by one of the sudden thunderstorms that frequently punctuated Georgia summer evenings.

"Whenever you're afraid, there's always Someone you can turn to," her mother had told the then five-year-old Olivia.

"You and Daddy," Olivia said confidently, secure now in her mother's arms.

"Daddy and I may not always be here," her mother said softly. "But the Lord will. Turn to Him. He'll never let you down."

Laura Hammond was gone less than a year later, taken by cancer. Olivia had often wondered if her mother had known even then that her time with her daughter would be limited and had wanted to teach her the importance of going to the Lord in prayer.

Olivia tucked the memories away to focus on the present. Though she'd felt a measure of peace after pouring out her heart to God, she was still gripped by paralyzing fear and the awful knowledge that she was responsible for getting Calvin back.

Sal had done some thinking of his own. Whoever took Calvin Chantry knew the man, knew what cases he was working on. Chances were that someone at the law firm was involved, at least peripherally.

Sal's lips narrowed at the thought of someone Olivia knew, someone she worked with, putting her through this. Whoever was behind this would pay.

He headed to Olivia's office, found her at her computer, a look of consternation on her face.

"I've written hundreds of briefs before. Why can't I write this one?"

The question didn't need an answer as they both knew why. "I want to do some snooping. I believe one or more of the people in your office is involved in this. The timing fits. It's the only thing that makes sense."

Olivia's denial wasn't as emphatic as he'd expected. He looked at her keenly, saw the doubt in her eyes. "You've already thought of it."

Her nod confirmed it. "You're right. I did. But I can't believe it. Calvin's like a father to everyone there. Many of the people have been here since my father was still alive."

"Think, Olivia." Sal kept his voice quiet but let a thread of steel run through it. "Someone had to know Chantry's schedule. Where and when they could snatch him. That means someone on the inside. Someone he trusted." Sal paused. "Someone you trust."

She pressed her fingertips to her eyes. "I can't believe it. We're family. We go to birthday parties for each other's children. We have a Christmas gift exchange and a Fourth of July barbecue."

Sal sighed. Time for a different tack. "You read the scriptures, right?"

Olivia nodded. "Every night."

"Then you know that they're full of stories of brothers killing brothers. Sons killing fathers. Cain and Abel come to mind."

"That's different." There was enough starch in her voice to iron a dozen shirts.

"Is it? Or is it only that you know the people at the office and like them?"

"Okay," she said, resentment filling her voice. "You win. Someone at the office may have had something to do with Calvin's kidnapping. How do we find out who it is?" And some of the starch evaporated.

"We're going to do a little digging. Ask a few questions. See if we make anyone nervous."

"How're we going to explain what you're doing there?"

"We stick to the truth as much as possible and tell everyone I'm here to make security upgrades."

"I guess that works."

"We'll make it work. This is our best chance." He took her hands, squeezed them gently before releasing them. "I can't promise that we'll get your boss back. But I can promise to do everything I can to make it happen."

She squared her shoulders. "If spying on my coworkers is what it takes to bring Calvin home safely, then that's what we'll do. It doesn't mean I have to like it." The starch was back.

"I didn't think you would."

FIVE

Olivia introduced Sal as a security expert.

"Bryan Hewston, Salvatore Santonni," she said to a colleague. "Bryan's one of the best litigators in the firm."

Bryan preened a bit. Olivia hadn't exaggerated. Bryan was a top-notch litigator in the boardroom and the court-room, but he relied too much on his charm without putting in the necessary work to back up his arguments.

It occasionally made for hard feelings, especially when she had been chosen as lead counsel on the pharmaceutical case over him. She knew he'd wanted the case, primarily for the publicity it would bring along with his part of the settlement, not because he believed in it.

She did. That was why she'd fought for it.

Bryan had been noticeably cool ever since Calvin had assigned the case to her. She'd shrugged it off. There would always be some in-fighting in a law office. She didn't have to like it to accept the reality of it.

Sal stuck out his hand and, after a brief hesitation, the other man took it. "Glad to meet you."

"Same here," Bryan said with his million-watt smile. The man had charisma by the boatload and knew how to use it. He was great with clients but, in her opinion at least, lacked the discipline to carry through with a case. "Look,

Olivia, if this case is too much for you to handle on your own, I can pitch in."

"No," she said quickly. "I'm fine."

He darted a doubtful look her way. She didn't blame him. A glance in the mirror that morning had confirmed what she already knew. Her naturally fair skin was now paper-white, her features pinched, her eyes like sunken sockets.

"You look a little peaked."

"Long nights," she said lightly.

She hoped the worry and fear didn't show in her voice. She wasn't adept at lying. Not that it was a skill she wanted to develop, but she occasionally wished that her face didn't broadcast her every feeling.

"Let me know if you decide you need help," he said and walked away.

Olivia bit back a sigh that hovered on her lips. It wasn't the first time he'd insinuated that the workload was too much for her. It probably wouldn't be the last.

Vicky Newman, another associate and full-time flirt, sashayed over. It didn't take her long, Olivia thought a bit waspishly, to zero in on Sal. She made the introductions, noting that Vicky made certain that Sal knew she was single within minutes of meeting him.

Though Olivia had nothing against the other woman, Vicky had been noticeably cool to Olivia ever since she had briefly dated a man Vicky was attracted to. In addition, Vicky, like Bryan, had resented that Olivia had been given the case against the drug company.

Olivia continued the casual introductions until Sal had met everyone, including the mail room delivery man.

"Seems like a decent bunch of people," he said when they ended up in her office.

"That's what I told you." She tried to keep the impatience from her voice, but some of it leaked through. "No

one here would hurt Calvin. Or me. It just isn't possible."
She had to believe that. If not, much of what she held dear
was false.

"I'm sorry this hurts you. But we have to look at every
possibility."

"Due diligence and all that. And I'm the one who's
sorry. I shouldn't have said what I did earlier. I lashed out
at you when you were only trying to help. It's just that
Calvin is special. If something happens to him…" Tears
stung her eyes, trickled down her cheeks. She swiped at
them. "Sorry. Crying isn't my style."

"I know." With that, Sal drew her to him in a one-sided
hug. His touch was gentle, but there was a quiet strength
to it, reminding her that he was a man a woman could lean
on. With that, she pulled away. She wasn't some helpless
woman needing a man. She'd always stood on her own
feet and intended on keeping it that way.

"Are you all right?"

"Yes." *No*.

"You don't have to be strong all the time," Sal said.
"Not with me."

He was wrong. She had always had to be strong. Especially around him.

Sal started with Hewston. He'd picked up on the lawyer's barely disguised antagonism toward Olivia.

Hewston was of average height and weight with features
that in another era would have been called patrician. He
had a tanned and toned look that spelled expensive ath-
letic clubs and time on the links.

His suit bore the quiet elegance of hand tailoring and
his shoes appeared to be Italian. Sal didn't care about
fancy clothes or shoes, but he'd learned enough about them
while working for S&J Security/Protection to recognize
the real thing.

But it wasn't Hewston's bespoke clothes or Bruno Maglis that interested Sal. It was the man's nervous energy that all but vibrated in the air, making Sal suspect the lawyer had something to hide.

The man studied Sal with frankly curious eyes. "So how do you know our Livvie?"

Sal raised a brow. He knew Olivia didn't share the nickname with many people. That this man used it so casually told Sal that Hewston intentionally wanted to convey a closeness that Sal had determined wasn't there, based on the coolness in Olivia's voice when she'd made the introductions. "We've known each other a few years."

"She's a great gal. A little emotional sometimes. You know women."

Sal didn't react to the obvious dig. Hewston clearly had his own agenda. You learned more by listening than talking, and so Sal let his silence encourage the other man to continue.

"Don't get me wrong. I like Livvie. I like her a lot. The whole office does."

"That's good to hear." Sal waited a beat. "She seems very fond of the head of the firm."

"Yeah. She and Chantry are tight. Nothing romantic, of course. Just good friends. He and her old man started the firm together back in the day."

"So she said." Sal nodded knowingly. "Must be nice to have a foot in the door, so to speak." His tone invited the other man to share.

"Yeah. And let me tell you, she isn't afraid of using her name to get what she wants. Take this case for instance."

"What about it?"

"Olivia wanted it, so Olivia got it. That simple." Bitterness twisted the man's lips.

"You don't think she earned it?"

"No way." Apparently wondering if he'd gone too far,

Hewston backpedaled. "I mean, she's a good enough lawyer, but a case that big needs someone with more experience."

"Someone like you?"

"Maybe." Modesty didn't sit well on the lawyer's shoulders. "There're other lawyers in the firm. Any one of us could have handled the case, but Olivia got it because her last name is Hammond." Resentment splashed through his voice. He couldn't hide his true feelings, Sal thought. Not for long.

"Does the rest of the firm feel the same way?" Sal asked.

Hewston darted a quick look around the office. "I couldn't say."

After a lot of thought, Olivia had come to the conclusion that Calvin's kidnapping had to be connected with the case against the pharmaceutical company. Otherwise, why take him at this particular time?

While Sal talked with her coworkers, she went through the files again, looking for something, anything, that would point to what made this case so important. Sure, the company would lose market shares and a chunk of money if a judgment were filed against it, but such things happened all the time. Other companies had weathered worse setbacks and rebounded.

Two hours later, she sat back and tried without success to rub the kinks from her shoulders. All she'd gotten for her efforts were strained eyes and knotted muscles. What had she expected to find? A big sign saying, "This is what you're looking for"?

Obviously she wasn't any good at this investigation stuff, and she hoped Sal had done better. She went in search of him and found him charming the receptionist.

"Thanks for chatting with me," he said, and the girl blushed prettily.

Olivia hooked her arm in his as they headed back to her office. "Did you learn anything?" she asked once they were inside with the door not only shut but locked as well. She normally didn't lock her door, but she didn't want anyone barging in on them while she and Sal were discussing the members of the firm.

"It seems that not everyone loves Chantry." Sal checked his notes. "According to a couple of the secretaries and a law clerk, Hewston made no secret of the fact that he thought Chantry was too old and set in his ways to lead the company."

Through the door's window she saw Bryan talking with one of the other associates. "Bryan was passed over for a partnership last year. For the third time. Rumor had it that he was ready to quit, but he didn't have anywhere to go. So he's still here."

"What do you think of him?"

"He's competent enough. Good at the grip-and-greet thing with clients, but he lacks follow-through."

Sal hiked a brow. "Not much of a recommendation."

"Bryan knows his stuff, but he tends to be lazy when it comes to doing the pre-trial work like looking up precedents and putting motions before the court."

"What about you? Do you mind that you're not a partner?"

"I'm not ready," she said easily. "Someday. When the time is right. In the meantime, I enjoy what I'm doing."

"Your father helped found the firm. That should count for something."

"It does. For him." She felt the familiar defenses slide into place. "I don't trade on my father's name. That's not who I am."

"No," Sal said. "It's not."

"Then why'd you ask?"

"I wanted to hear you say it."

They spent the next hour going over Sal's impressions of the office personnel with Olivia filling in details where she could.

"What about Newman? She looks hungry. Like she wants whatever someone else has."

"Hungry's a good way to describe her. She's poached other people's clients when she could. But kidnapping?" Olivia stopped, thought about it. "Maybe. She hasn't made a secret of the fact that she wants to be more than an associate."

"You know these people. Know what makes them tick. Would any of them be willing to sell out Chantry for a big payday?"

"I don't want to believe it. But maybe…" She thought of the designer bags that Vicky carried to work, the flashy car that Bryan drove. Neither of them could afford those on their salaries. "They might."

Sal nodded. "I thought so. I spotted the Kate Spade bag."

Olivia couldn't contain her spurt of surprise. "You know Kate Spade handbags?"

"I have three sisters. They'll live on ramen soup for six months if it means they can buy a genuine Kate Spade. Our brother, Nicco, calls them purse snobs."

She heard the amusement in the words, but there was more. There was real love, causing her to recall her childhood wish for a sister. Or a brother. It hadn't mattered.

"You're fortunate to have your sisters and brother."

"We Santonnis are a loud, bossy bunch. I'll take you to meet them one day—" He stopped abruptly.

He was remembering the same thing she was, she thought, a pang of regret spearing through her. Two years ago, they'd planned a trip to meet his family.

It had never happened.

"What about you?" he asked. "Are you into designer handbags?"

Olivia shook her head and patted her battered briefcase. "Daddy gave this to me when I graduated from law school. It's getting pretty beat-up, but I always carry it." Her voice caught. "It reminds me of him.

"I have to get back to work," she said, the huskiness of her voice at odds with the teasing note of earlier.

"Yeah. And I should be talking with more of your coworkers. See what I can learn."

He closed the door behind him, leaving Olivia feeling more alone than ever. Without her knowing how it had happened, Sal was starting to become important to her all over again. The question was, what was she going to do about it?

SIX

By the end of the day, Sal had a pretty good handle on Chantry & Hammond's personnel. There was the flirt. The jealous coworker. The ambitious partners. For the most part, they fit neatly into categories.

He'd do background checks on each, including any criminal history. It wasn't difficult to figure out that several members of the law firm were living beyond their means.

He'd zeroed in on Bryan Hewston and Vicky Newman. A call to Shelley netted him the information that Newman came from money and had a substantial trust fund. Okay, that explained the designer bags and clothes. Hewston was another matter. It wasn't clear, Shelley told him, where his money came from. She promised to do more digging.

"Thanks, boss."

"Take care of Olivia. From what you've said, she's in over her head."

"You know I will."

"I wish I could be there, but I can hardly tie my own shoes, much less chase down bad guys."

Sal gave the expected chuckle, but his mind wasn't really on what Shelley was saying. He was too busy trying to convince himself that he didn't still have feelings for Olivia, before giving it up as a lost cause. Mixing personal and private matters was a recipe for disaster, so he was determined to keep things strictly professional.

That was the way to go. The only way to go.

He'd insisted on accompanying her to the Savannah courthouse and seeing her home at the end of the day. In between chatting up her coworkers, he'd found a motel, stashed his duffel bag there. He could have stayed at his parents' place or with his brother, Nicco, but he preferred having the freedom of movement that a motel room offered.

Though he'd grown up in Savannah, he'd kept his distance from his family since his return from Afghanistan. The past kept tripping him up. He'd hidden the darker parts from his family as well as Olivia.

He knew he needed to make time to see his family. Until then, he contented himself with a phone call to his parents, assuring them that he was all right and would see them once the case was resolved.

He now waited at the side entrance to the courthouse as they'd agreed.

Heels clicking on the marble floor, Olivia made her way to where he stood. He took in the defeated expression on her face.

"A setback in court?"

"Waterloo was a setback. This was a disaster." She tried a smile, but it barely made it to her lips. "I let everyone down." Her shoulders slumped. "Especially the parents. They're depending on me."

"You're too hard on yourself. Always tilting at windmills."

"That's what windmills are for."

He understood that defending the underdog was what had made her want to be a lawyer in the first place. "You'll get 'em tomorrow."

"I hope so. I have to." Her voice hardened. "What the

company did to those children is as good as murder. And that's what I'll take it down for."

From what he'd heard about the case against the pharmaceutical company, the parents filing the suit stood a good chance of winning. His eyes narrowed at the thought of sick children being given counterfeit drugs.

Children had always held a special place in his heart. He doted on his nieces and nephews and took every chance he had to spoil them, much to his sisters' chagrin. While in Afghanistan, he'd taken a special interest in the children and had the nickname Gentle Giant bestowed upon him. He sent most of his salary from S&J to a foundation that helped children displaced by war.

"You're a real hard case, Hammond, you know that?"

This time her smile reached her eyes. "So I've heard."

"I like that in a woman."

"Why, thank you, kind sir." Her eyelashes fluttered flirtatiously. "But I do declare that you've made me blush."

The back-and-forth felt good. The time with Olivia had been punctuated with threats, fear and worry. They needed to step back occasionally and remember the normal.

"Come on. I'll take you to dinner."

"Could we pick up something and take it home? I want to get out of these heels and put my feet up."

"You're the boss."

He stopped for burgers and fries, the enticing smell of grilled beef wafting through the truck's cab. Olivia was probably as hungry as he was, and he drove a bit faster to meet her at her townhome. Once they had both reached her place, Olivia excused herself, murmuring that she wanted to change out of her suit.

She reappeared five minutes later dressed in a soft pink track suit, hair pulled back in a long ponytail. To his eyes, she was even more beautiful than she had been in the spit and polish of the professional suit. She looked as fresh as a bowl of strawberry ice cream.

He was wondering how to prepare her for the possibility that they might not be able to get her boss back when she brought up the subject.

"You don't think we'll get Calvin back alive."

He didn't answer right away, wanting to choose his words with care. "I don't know what to think." That was honest. "Remember that it's not just Calvin's life on the line," he felt compelled to add. "The kidnappers have you in their sights as well." He knew that she was less afraid for herself than she was for her boss.

That was Olivia—always putting others first.

Sal tightened his lips. It was up to him to make certain she didn't become a casualty.

Olivia checked her watch for what seemed the hundredth time in the last hour. "Why don't they call?" Waiting was hard, brutally hard. "I just want to get it over with."

"They're depending on that. When they do call, they want you so shaken that you'll do exactly as they say."

"Of course I'll do what they say." There was no question of that.

"We have to get the upper hand somehow."

"And how would we do that?"

"We find out all we can about your boss. What he's been doing the last few months. Who he's seen. Everything."

"Calvin does his own thing. He mostly leaves the day-to-day tasks to the partners and associates."

"Then why kidnap him?"

The question they'd asked themselves over and over.

"You don't know what you're getting yourself into."

"I have to do this. Calvin is depending on me." She had to see this through. For Calvin's sake as well as her own. "I shouldn't have involved you."

"You can't do this on your own." A deep line of annoyance rode between his brows.

She bristled. "Thanks for the vote of confidence."

Despite her tart words, she found herself wanting to lean on him in ways that were far from acceptable. With more regret than she expected, she pushed away.

"Sorry. I didn't mean you weren't capable in most things, only that you're out of your league here."

"Is that supposed to make me feel better?"

"It's supposed to make you think smart."

She was responsible for getting Calvin back safely. The kidnappers' call had been very clear about that.

Olivia reached for another fry. Sal did the same, their fingers brushing each other fleetingly. She fought the twin urges to pull back and to prolong the touch. In the end, she took a fry and pretended she hadn't noticed the jolt of electricity that had arced between them. A glance at his face told her that he, too, was not unaffected.

Her gaze drifted to where their hands had oh-so-briefly met before she'd pulled away and busied herself with the fries. The subtle deepening of the lines bracketing his mouth wasn't lost on her; nor was the tightening of his shoulders. He'd seen through her charade of pretending she hadn't noticed the sparks.

She wanted to explain, to apologize, but feared that doing so would only draw attention to what was best ignored. Acting on that momentary awareness that had flashed from his hand to hers could only lead to regret. She had enough regret regarding Sal without heaping more on to it.

A smart woman would keep her distance and remind herself that he was only there to help her get Calvin back safely. She'd always considered herself a smart woman.

Now she wondered.

SEVEN

After seeing Olivia to the courthouse in the morning, Sal went back to digging into the law firm's employees.

Nothing sent up a red flag on anyone except Hewston. The lawyer seemed to have money to spare and Sal wanted to know where it came from. When in doubt, follow the money. It was a tried-and-true investigative technique.

He knew his way around a computer, but Shelley was better at unearthing things people wanted to keep hidden. A lot better.

It occurred to him that he needed to find out more about Calvin Chantry as well as his employees. If the kidnapping had to do with the case Olivia was trying, why kidnap Chantry? Why not Olivia? Everything came back to the *why* of it.

Sal could only be grateful that it hadn't been Olivia who had been taken, Olivia who had been subjected to the fear and pain that Chantry had endured.

When she called to say that the defense had asked for a recess for the rest of the day, Sal told her to stay put and that he'd pick her up. Though she seemed to have recovered from the scare of two men holding her at knifepoint, images of that remained stuck in his mind.

He pulled up at the side entrance to the courthouse. Olivia saw him and waved. Just as she started toward him, two men grabbed her. Sal tore out of the truck and ran to where she struggled with the would-be abductors. She fought valiantly and got in several good kicks, but she was no match for the burly men who tried to force her into a van illegally parked on the side street.

Sal drove his fist in the gut of one man, sending him sprawling to the sidewalk. The other leveled a Walther at Sal's chest, the barrel touching his sternum at point-blank range. Sal didn't hesitate, slamming the side of his hand against the man's forearm. The assailant opened his hand reflexively, dropping the gun, and shot a look of hatred at Sal. His partner scooped up the weapon, and the two of them took off.

Olivia hurried to Sal. "Are you okay?"

He wasn't surprised that her first thought was for him rather than herself. That was Olivia, always putting others first. "Fine. What about you?"

"Shaky. But okay." Hair pulled from its neat French twist and her suit torn, Olivia still managed to look beautiful. "Who were they?"

"That's what I was going to ask you. Could they be the same men who broke into your office?"

"I don't know. Their builds were similar. They didn't say anything, so I can't identify voices, but—" she paused "—they smelled the same."

"Smelled?"

"Like fish." She wrinkled her nose. "Stale fish."

Sal bundled her into his truck.

"Don't tell me," she said once her seat belt was fastened. "We've got another trip to the police station in our future."

"'Fraid so."

At the precinct, they explained what had happened to Detective Nynan, who had taken their earlier report. "You folks sure attract trouble."

"Yeah," Sal said. "We're trying to work on that."

After they'd signed their statements and Detective Nynan had briefed them on what the police had uncovered, which wasn't much, Olivia and Sal headed back to where he had parked his truck.

Because he needed to reassure himself that Olivia was all right, he wrapped his arm around her shoulders, to comfort both her and him.

She turned to face him. "Thank you for showing up when you did."

"That was too close." Pictures of what the men might have done to Olivia if they'd managed to get her in the van swirled through his mind.

"I'm okay." She studied him, must have seen the worry in his eyes. "Just remember that our priority is finding Calvin."

Sal didn't disagree, but he knew where his priorities lay: keeping Olivia safe. He'd do whatever it took.

When Olivia learned that Sal had wanted to visit Calvin's house but planned to take her home instead, she objected. "I'm fine. My suit will never be the same, but the rest of me is good. If you taking a look at Calvin's house helps us find him, that's what we'll do. What are you looking for?"

"I want to get a feel for the man. How he lives. Anything that might give us a clue as to who might have it in for him."

She gave directions to Calvin's house in one of Savannah's exclusive suburbs, all the while wondering if they'd been off base in assuming Calvin's kidnapping was tied to the case against the pharmaceutical company.

Could he have stumbled on something in another case that put him at risk? He hadn't told her of anything even remotely dangerous, but if it was serious enough to have someone abduct him, he was probably keeping it to himself in a misguided effort to protect her.

Calvin's house was a pseudo Southern-style mansion. She'd often teased him that he was born a century too late because he embraced everything about the old South. When he'd discovered that he couldn't buy the genuine article, he'd built his own ostentatious version of a stately home, complete with driveways made from crushed shells and wrought-iron balconies that wrapped around the second story of the house.

The effect was overwhelming and more than a bit ostentatious.

Olivia had never had the heart to tell him that the house fell short of the mark. It screamed bad taste and new money, a deadly combination in Savannah society. A century and a half ago, he'd have been called a carpetbagger. Now people sneered at him behind his back.

Calvin had never let on that it bothered him. Instead, he kept making money. She'd once asked him where all the money came from, and he'd only smiled and said, "Smart investing."

"It's…different," Sal said at last as he took in the massive columns, the overdone portico, the black shutters against the painted brick.

"Old-timers call it 'that carpetbagger's house.'"

He smothered a laugh. "Good one."

"Okay, so Calvin went a bit overboard with the whole Tara theme. But it has its charm."

Sal's raised brow invited her to identify that charm. She thought, trying to come up with something. "The grounds are gorgeous. He has a staff of gardeners who work year round to keep everything pristine."

"Too bad they can't fix bad taste."

Silently, she agreed. Understatement was not one of Calvin's traits. The bigger, the better, had always been his motto, but he took pleasure in his home, and that was enough. He also gave lavishly to the cultural arts and was on the boards of several of the most prominent charities in Savannah.

"What do you expect to find here?"

"I don't know," Sal answered. "Something more than what we have."

She was welcomed into the mansion by the housekeeper, Bessie.

"Bessie," Olivia said and leaned forward to kiss the woman's cheek. "Bessie Raymond, meet Sal Santonni."

"Pleased to meet you, sir." Bessie turned her attention to Olivia. "Bless you, Ms. Hammond. It's that glad I am to see you. I haven't heard hide nor hair from Mr. Chantry in three days."

"Does Mr. Chantry usually let you know when he's going to be out of town?" Sal asked casually.

"Yes. Very considerate that way, Mr. Chantry is."

"Could we take a look inside Mr. Chantry's study?" Olivia asked. "I need to pick up some papers for work."

"Well, I suppose that'd be okay."

Olivia led Sal to the study. Two stories in height, it was her favorite room in the house. Paneled in cypress wood, it was warmly decorated in tones of gold and hunter green and promised hours of reading delight with the requisite sliding ladder attached to the shelves of books occupying three walls.

She moved to Calvin's desk. Calvin was meticulous in his organizing, and his desk reflected that. Nothing seemed out of place. Neither did anything appear missing. She had been here enough to recognize the precise placement of the blotter, the pen-and-pencil set, the Venetian glass paperweight that had never held down any papers.

"I don't know what I'm looking for," she said in frustration.

"Anything that looks like it doesn't belong. Or anything that should be here that isn't."

A leather desk set. A letter opener and scissors in silver. A stack of files neatly arranged in alphabetical order. The brass figurine—where was it?

She opened the drawers, didn't see it.

"What are you looking for?"

"A miniature brass. It was a favorite of Calvin's. He'd found it in an antiques shop. Cerberus."

"Cerberus? As in the three-headed beast?"

She nodded.

"Is it valuable?"

She furrowed her brow, trying to recall the details of the tiny statue. "Not particularly. I think he bought it on a whim."

"Would he have moved it?"

"Not that I know of. But…maybe." She certainly didn't know everything about Calvin's home. Maybe he'd moved the figurine to his bedroom. Or the front room.

"Anything else out of place or missing?" Sal asked.

"No." The missing figurine was hardly proof of anything. It certainly didn't help them in finding Calvin. "Let me say goodbye to Bessie and then we can go."

"Sure."

Olivia found Bessie in the foyer, polishing the gleaming balustrade. "Thank you, Bessie, for allowing us in."

"I'm prayin' I'll be hearin' from Mr. Calvin soon," the woman said, twisting a cloth.

"I'm sure you will." Olivia paused. "I noticed that the little statue on Calvin's desk wasn't there. Did he move it to another room?"

"I'm sure he didn't. Many's the time he said he liked to look at it while he was at his desk workin'." A stricken look settled on the housekeeper's face. "You're not sayin' I took it, are you, Ms. Hammond?"

"No! No, of course not. I just wondered. The desk looked empty without it."

"Well, all right then."

Olivia and Sal took their leave. Outside, he turned to her. "What was that all about?"

"Something about the Cerberus being missing bothers me." She lifted a shoulder. "I don't know why."

"Does Chantry have children?"

She nodded. "A son. Walter."

"Do you think he'd know anything?"

"I don't know. Walter's an investment banker. Hey," she said when Sal gave a slight sneer. "Don't knock it. He's an ex-SEAL. You and he could probably swap war stories."

"A SEAL-turned-investment banker. An odd fit."

"I don't know. From what I hear, the financial world is pretty cutthroat." She pulled out her phone. "Let me call, see if he's home."

The drive to Walter's condo took twenty minutes. Olivia used the time to try to figure out what was going on between her and Sal. She could no longer deny the sizzle of awareness whenever they were in the same room.

Walter Chantry's condo sat on a pricey piece of land with its own boardwalk that stretched out to the bay. In the drive was a Land Rover LR3. With a supercharged Jaguar engine under the hood, the vehicle had probably set Walter back a hundred thousand dollars or so.

Sal gave a low whistle. "Investment banking must pay well."

"Walter has always been a go-getter. Even when we were kids, he had schemes going. He was always looking for the next big thing."

"You and he close?"

"We spent time together as children, but as we got older, we grew apart. He's a couple of years older than I am, and he went off to college, then joined the navy. When he came back a few years ago, he was already well-off. He's done really well for himself."

"Sounds like Walter has found his place in life."

"I'd say so." As she thought about it, she reflected that father and son weren't particularly close. Certainly not as close as she and her father had been, but there was no crime in that.

When Walter answered his door, Olivia made the introductions. Sal extended his hand, and, after a moment, Walter took it. The handshake lasted at least thirty seconds longer than necessary, as though each man was testing the other's strength.

It would have been comical, but they weren't laughing. Neither was Olivia.

"Chantry."

"Santonni."

The two men sized each other up. They were both physically fit, both big and strong, but to her eye, Walter came up short. It had nothing to do with size and everything to do with being comfortable in one's own skin.

Sal didn't have anything to prove, she realized, whereas Walter was always trying to impress someone. Maybe that was why they'd stopped getting together.

"Walter, we wondered if you'd heard from your father lately."

Walter looked surprised. "No. But we're not much on talking on the phone. Sometimes we get together to go hunting or fishing. Any special reason you're asking?"

She hesitated, snuck a look at Sal. Imperceptibly, he shook his head. "No. He took a few days off, and there's something at the office that needs his attention." She winced at the weak explanation.

But Walter didn't seem to notice anything off. "If I hear from him, I'll tell him to give you a call. Good enough?"

"Sure. Thanks." She turned to leave, paused. "Walter..."

"Yes?"

"Thanks for seeing us," Olivia said easily. "I appreciate the time."

"No problem."

Outside, she rounded on Sal. "Why didn't you want me to say anything? He has a right to know that his father's been kidnapped."

"I don't know what to think. I just don't want to give away anything. Not yet."

Walter? A kidnapper?

The thought startled her, but before she could push it totally out of her mind, she considered it. Granted, she and Walter had grown apart over the last decade or so. He wanted different things from life than she did. Again, no crime in that.

His obsession with material things had always been a stumbling block between them. Even as a kid, Walter had had to have the most expensive sneakers, the computer with all the bells and whistles. She'd seen it as amusing at first before his obsession had grown to include the Ferrari sports car, designer clothes and a Rolex.

But to kidnap his own father? It was laughable. What would he gain by it? "Investment banking's where the big boys play," he'd said more than once.

He and Calvin had a different kind of relationship than the one she and her father had shared. Theirs seemed to be one of competition, but it worked for them, so who was she to criticize?

"You don't like him," she said.

"I don't not like him. I'm reserving judgment."

"What does that mean?"

"Just that. I don't know him, so I can't make any judgment. Yet."

The last word hung in the air. "Why can't you take anyone at face value?"

"Maybe because I've seen too many people who wear too many faces." Sal placed his hands on either side of her face. "Not you. Never you. Everything you are is right out front. But not everyone is like you."

"I don't know what to say."

"Just say that you'll be careful. We're dealing with too many unknowns."

EIGHT

Sal always knew how to figure out a problem. It was a Salvatore Santonni way of life. He was good at working his way around obstacles. So why was he coming up at dead ends with this op?

That's how he thought of protecting Olivia and rescuing Chantry: an op. No different from any other he and his Delta unit had pulled off in the Middle East countless times. Only this was Olivia's life. That changed the stakes.

The clink of silverware against the china stirred him from his thoughts, reminding him that he wasn't alone. Olivia sat across the table from him, her eyes dark with concern.

He'd insisted they eat at a real restaurant the following night. They'd both needed a break from the diet of fast food and worry. "Sorry," he said briefly. "My thoughts took a detour."

"No problem."

At that moment, the two men sitting three tables over caught his attention. It wasn't anything they did. It was more a matter of how they held themselves. There was a watchfulness to them that set them apart from the other diners.

To anyone who had served in the armed forces or with the police, the hypervigilant posture was unmistakable. Neither man had touched his drink. Nor had they taken their gaze from Olivia and himself. Both wore button-down shirts with the sleeves rolled up, revealing thick arms ropey with muscles.

Sal clicked into combat mode. He didn't doubt that he could take them. They appeared to be in reasonably good shape, but they looked a little soft around the edges, as though it had been a while since they'd seen active duty. It had been several years since Sal had left Delta, but he hadn't let civilian life interfere with his staying in shape. Daily ten-mile runs and lifting weights kept him fit.

But he had Olivia to think of. She wasn't a combatant. Putting her in danger wasn't an option, but how was he supposed to get them past the men who would undoubtedly stake out the entrance to the restaurant?

The rear door led to an alley that could become its own trap if the men had some confederates watching it. Ex-military types like he'd pegged the men to be often operated as part of a unit. It was entirely possible that another team was waiting at the back door, ready to ambush him and Olivia. Alleys could become death traps, the canyon-like walls providing surfaces from which bullets could ricochet.

However much he didn't want to take Olivia out the front door, he didn't see he had a choice.

Without more intel, he had to make the best decision he could under the circumstances. His mind sifted through the various possibilities, and he still came up with the same plan of action.

He made no secret of his study of the men and raised his glass, not in a toast but in acknowledgment of their presence. In his experience, it did no good to feign ignorance of the enemy. Better to let them know they'd been spotted. The knowledge might rattle them.

It became a matter of who blinked first.

Surprise crossed the face of the smaller of the two men before he started to return the gesture. He was stopped by the other. Okay. The roles had been established. Leader. Subordinate. Sal filed that away. It was helpful to know who was giving the orders and who was following them.

Sal didn't miss the silent exchange between the two men. The leader slapped a couple of bills on the table, got up. After a slight hesitation, his partner did the same.

"What's going on?" Olivia asked as the men walked out. "Why were you watching those men?"

"Because they were watching us. When we go outside, stay behind me. When I say move, you move."

She didn't bother protesting but only nodded.

Sal took his time paying the check. He wanted to let the men get in position. If they felt they had the advantage, they were likely to be overconfident. With Olivia at his side and slightly behind him, they exited the restaurant.

He could have called 911, told the police what was happening, but what did he have to go on besides a couple of men in a restaurant looking at him and Olivia? Plus, he wanted to question the men. If they had anything to do with Chantry's kidnapping, Sal needed to know.

He thought of telling Olivia to hang back, but he knew better. She wasn't one to run.

Her grip on his arm tightened as they left the brightly lit building and the dark Georgia night closed in around them.

"It'll be okay," he said.

Before he'd gotten out the last word, the bigger of the two men, the one Sal had pegged as the leader, stepped in front of him. "We got a message for you. You and your lady are making certain people nervous. Real nervous. In fact, they're so nervous that they want us to teach you a lesson."

"Care to enlighten us as to who those people are?" Sal asked, angling himself between Olivia and the men.

"It don't matter," the second man said.

To Sal's chagrin, Olivia stepped out from behind him.

"The lady," she said with emphasis, "can take care of herself."

The second man grabbed her arms, held them behind her back. "You sure about that?"

Sal ground his teeth together. Anger that the man had put his hands on Olivia ran hot. No man, no real man, hurt a woman. He started toward the thug, intending on giving him a lesson in manners, when Olivia slammed her heel on the man's instep.

The move, though simple, was effective, and Sal silently applauded. At the same time, he wished she'd done as he'd ordered. They'd talk about that. Later. First, he had to take care of the other thug.

Howling, the man who'd held Olivia released her. At that moment, the larger man advanced on Sal, raising a meaty fist. He was big but was starting to go to fat.

Sal didn't retreat but instead moved in. Taken off guard, his assailant made a misstep. Sal let the man's momentum carry him to the asphalt where he landed with a thud. Using the enemy's energy against himself was the oldest trick in the book.

The man didn't stay down, though. He pushed himself up, came at Sal with both fists raised, and got in a punch, splitting Sal's lip.

Sal returned the volley with a shot of his own, hitting the man in the jaw. The big guy rubbed at his jaw. First surprise, then anger registered on his face. "The boss said not to kill you, but he didn't say we couldn't make you hurt."

"Oh? How're you going to do that?" Sal had been watching the man and noticed that he telegraphed his moves by wetting his lips. Sal slid a leg out, caught the man off guard. He fell to the ground a second time.

"This ain't over," the smaller man said, hobbling on his good foot and shooting angry darts at Olivia.

"Tell your boss to send some real men next time," she said.

The larger man glared at her. "Sister, you better hope there ain't a next time. 'Cuz you won't like it."

Sal had had enough. He slammed his fist into his opponent's gut, followed up with a slice with the back of his hand to the man's neck.

The smaller of the pair charged at Sal. Sal easily deflected the head butt. He wanted to finish the fight then and there, but he needed to get Olivia away from here even more. She was going to crash and burn after the initial surge of adrenaline wore off.

Eyes shining, Olivia pumped a fist in the air. "Guess we showed them." The exhilaration in her voice was in stark contrast to her earlier fear.

Sal wanted to share in her triumph, but he had a bad feeling. Whoever sent the muscle after him and Olivia obviously had money and connections. It made sense that this was connected with Chantry's kidnapping, but what if it was something else altogether?

He had been turning over rocks in the last couple of days. It looked like a snake had been hiding beneath one of them.

"Did the men look familiar?" Sal asked once they'd gotten back to Olivia's place. "Could they be the ones who attacked you?"

She knew he was trying to make connections between the attacks but reluctantly shook her head as she tended his split lip. "No. The men in the office wore masks, but their builds were different. So were their voices."

She studied her handiwork, decided it would do. "For having sent those idiots on their way with their tails between their legs, you don't look very happy."

Sal rubbed the back of his neck. "The guy you almost crippled—good move by the way—was right. Whoever sent them is probably going to send more men after us. And they won't be so easy to take down."

"Why do you think they were after us? Because of Calvin?"

"Could be. Or it could be something else entirely. We've been stirring things up at your office."

Her response was emphatic. "Nobody there has reason to hurt me."

"Sure about that?"

"Of course…" Her voice dwindled away. Bryan had been making noises that her pro bono work was cutting into the firm's profits, but that wasn't reason enough to send a couple of thugs after her. Was it?

"What?" Sal persisted.

"Bryan. I can't imagine he'd be involved in something like this, but he's never really been a fan of mine." She made a face. "In fact, he'd like nothing better than if I quit the firm. He's never said it out loud, but it's there." She explained about the pro bono clients. "Daddy and Calvin set up the firm so that even associates get a share of the profits. More than once, Bryan's accused me of taking money out of his pocket so I can play do-gooder."

Sal muttered something uncomplimentary about the lawyer under his breath. "We need to take a second look at him."

"Bryan wouldn't have any reason to kidnap Calvin."

"Money's always a motive. You said yourself that there was lots of money involved with the lawsuit. You never know what someone is willing to do until push comes to shove."

She thought about it. Sal was right. She'd never imagined herself in a fight outside a bar. For the last two years, she'd been taking lessons in martial arts. They'd finally paid off.

He must have read her thoughts. "You handled yourself

like a pro back there. Kept your cool and didn't let them intimidate you. Where'd you learn that move?"

"Do you remember when those men tried to rob us two years ago? You took care of it, and I stood around like a helpless female. I decided that I wasn't going to be helpless again and started taking lessons at a dojo. So, you get some of the credit."

Sal grinned. "I don't remember using my high heel."

She laughed. "Maybe not. That was my idea. The instructor said to use what's available. I figured my high heel was as good a weapon as any." She couldn't help it. She gave another fist pump. "It's my first bar fight. Or almost bar fight."

"I'd have never known," he said straight-faced and gave her a hug. She leaned into it. Into him.

"It felt good. That guy will be limping for days." There, with Sal's arms around her, she remembered how good it felt to be held by him. She lifted her head, let her gaze meet his.

He lowered his head and touched his lips to hers in a kiss so sweet that it brought tears to her eyes.

When he ended the kiss, she knew an acute sense of loss. "I'm sorry. That shouldn't have happened."

He kissed her and then apologized? Any tenderness she might have felt evaporated.

"Those guys were hired muscle," Sal said, as if he'd forgotten the kiss already. "Where there's two, there're likely more. I don't know if they're connected to taking your boss, but you have to know that kidnappings rarely have a happy ending."

Her annoyance of a few minutes ago died as she absorbed Sal's words. "You're trying to prepare me for the worst. I get it. But we don't have any evidence to suggest that Calvin isn't still alive. I'm going with that. I have to."

If she didn't have hope to cling to, she didn't think she could keep going.

She pulled away from him, reminding herself that falling for Sal again would jeopardize not only her heart but her sanity as well.

She wanted to tell him how she felt. At the same time, she shied away from putting her feelings into words. How would he react? Would he run in the opposite direction? Or would he understand that her feelings were all too real?

Sal breathed in deeply. Again. The deliberate motion helped to slow the adrenaline that continued to course through him.

Bit by bit, his body relaxed from its battle-ready tension. The tension was an invisible suit of armor soldiers donned when facing danger. The act was so ingrained as to go almost unnoticed, but the loosening of the muscles and the hyperawareness were unmistakable.

The body couldn't sustain an adrenaline rush for extended periods of time. Too much energy, both physical and emotional, was needed to keep it up. Soldiers, especially those in special ops, learned to make the transition.

At the same time, he was struggling with his reaction to Olivia's nearness and her response to his kiss. Kissing her had been incredibly stupid, no doubt about it, but he'd been unable to help himself.

There was no future for them. Not future at all. He hadn't been honest with her, and without honesty, love withered and died.

"You must think I'm pretty foolish, acting like I'm some kind of kickboxing champion just because I got in one good hit," Olivia said.

"No. You did good." He let her take that in before continuing. "But next time, if there is a next time, you move when I say move." He saw that she was going to object to that and hurried on. "Now we have to decide what to do next."

"Finding out who hired Tweedledee and Tweedledum?"

"Yeah. I managed to grab a button from the big guy's shirt. S&J has contacts in the PD. We'll get an ID on his prints and go from there."

"Not bad, Santonni."

"We aim to please, ma'am."

His smile was indulgent. Olivia was riding high right now. She'd fall soon enough. He'd be there to catch her when she did.

It happened sooner than he'd thought. One minute she was talking, the next she'd grown silent. And why hadn't he noticed how pale she'd turned, how dark her eyes had grown? He'd been looking for the signs of adrenaline-fueled exhaustion, but he'd missed the most obvious ones.

"Come on," he said. "You're falling down tired."

"I guess I am. I wasn't…and now I am." The surprise in her voice made him want to smile. As tough as Olivia thought herself to be, she was an innocent in the dark world of kidnappings and brawls. When would she figure that out?

In the meantime, it was his job to take care of her when she refused to take care of herself.

"I'll overnight the button to Shelley."

"How soon do you think you'll hear back?"

"Maybe the day after tomorrow."

Her sigh of disappointment matched his own. They needed answers now.

NINE

The next morning, Sal made a quick call to Shelley. After making sure she'd received the button he'd sent, he got down to business. "What have you found in Hewston's background?"

"Not much. Yet. You think he's behind the kidnapping?"

"I don't know. But something about him is off." Sal proceeded to tell her about last night's ambush.

"Are you and Olivia okay?"

"We're good." A smile slid over his lips as he thought of Olivia's pride in scoring a hit on her opponent.

"One more thing," Shelley said. "And knowing you, you've already thought of it. It's what, day three or more since Olivia's boss was taken?"

Sal knew where she was going with this. "We're running out of time to get Chantry back alive."

Shelley didn't say anything more. She didn't have to.

A small groan sounded over the phone.

"What's wrong?" Sal asked in quick concern. Not only was Shelley his boss, she was the little sister of his best friend.

"Nothing that having this baby won't fix. I think he's playing soccer—" another groan "—for both teams. Caleb," she said, referring to her husband, "is in worse shape than

I am. You'd think a big bad Delta could handle one little pregnancy, wouldn't you?"

"Cut him some slack," Sal advised, chuckling over Caleb Judd, a much-decorated Delta, struggling with his wife's pregnancy. "Delta training didn't cover pregnancy."

Shelley's answering laugh told him that she was enjoying her husband's discomfort. "I'll get back to you on Hewston as soon as I can."

"Thanks. And take care, little mama." There was real affection in the words.

"You, too." She paused. "How's Olivia?"

Now it was Sal's turn to pause. "Okay."

"That's all? Just okay?" The words held expectancy.

She was more than okay. But Sal couldn't tell his boss that. He couldn't tell anyone how he felt about Olivia when he didn't know himself.

An hour later, Shelley called back. "I struck gold on Bryan Hewston. He's in debt to online gaming sites to the tune of two hundred and fifty thousand dollars. He's been embezzling from Chantry & Hammond for three years. I called some CIs in Savannah. Turns out Hewston's in hock all over town and has some mean types breathing down his neck."

Sal nodded. Shelley had a network of confidential informants throughout the South.

It wasn't much of a stretch, Shelley continued, to discover that he had connections to a few ex-military types who would do anything for money. At that, Sal's lips narrowed. He and his buddies had served America with honor and pride, some of them making the ultimate sacrifice with their lives.

Fury filled him at the idea of anyone using their training for ignoble purposes. It tarnished the name and reputation of every good man and woman who had served, past and present.

With an effort, he pushed his anger aside and did what he did best: confront the enemy. That this enemy wore three-piece suits and spent his days in an office rather than the mountains of Afghanistan didn't change the hunt.

Sal was an apex predator. He waited for Hewston outside the law firm. When his quarry emerged, Sal followed him to a nearby watering hole that catered to young professionals. Sal slid beside Hewston in a booth, effectively trapping the lawyer.

"You sent those thugs after us. Why?" Sal knew the answer; he just wanted to see what the man would say.

Would he flat-out deny the charge? Or would he come clean and confess? Sal didn't have much confidence in the latter. Everything he'd learned about Hewston said the man was weak, took the easy way out whenever possible and blamed others for his poor choices.

"I don't know what you're talking about," the lawyer blustered, confirming Sal's prediction. Sal sighed. Sometimes he hated being right.

"And I don't appreciate the accusation," Hewston said, a sneer in his voice and his mouth curling in a scowl. "Did Olivia put you up to this? She's always had it in for me." Righteous indignation coated every syllable, but fear shadowed his eyes. He squirmed in the booth, eyes darting in all directions as he sought a way out.

"Knock it off. I know you were the one who hired them, so you might as well spill it."

Before Hewston could register another protest, Sal cut him off. "Don't bother lying. I've got the goods on you and have already shared everything with the Savannah PD."

The arrogance in the man's eyes slowly faded away as he finally absorbed that he wasn't going to bluff his way out of this, and, like a balloon losing its air, Hewston deflated. "I knew you were looking at me. It was only a matter of time until you'd find out what I was doing."

"Embezzling from the firm's clients."

"Yeah." The sizzle had fled, and his expression was that of a spoiled kid who'd just had all his toys stolen by someone bigger. "I couldn't let it go that far. I'd lose my license, maybe even go to jail. I was just trying to buy some time." There was no remorse in his voice, only resentment.

"So you thought you'd scare us off." Sal didn't bother pointing out that the man's debts weren't going to go away with a little time.

A jerky nod was the only answer.

"They could have killed Olivia," Sal said, anger vibrating in every syllable. "Was covering up your habit worth that?"

"I told them not to kill her. Just rough her up a bit. I only wanted to make the two of you stop looking into my business." Hewston offered the explanation as though that excused what he'd done.

"That's how you solve your mess? By roughing up an innocent woman?" Sal had to stop himself from yanking the man out of the booth to show him just what he could do in the roughing-up department. He fisted his hands on the table, giving Hewston a hint of what he wanted to do.

The lawyer shrank back in his seat, all bravado gone.

"You're going away, buddy. If I have my way, it'll be for a long, long time."

Sal had no sympathy for people who cheated their way through life. According to him, it was laziness that motivated them, laziness and greed. "We've already established that you're a cheat and a liar. Are you also a kidnapper?"

"Are you crazy?"

"Like you don't know. Calvin Chantry's been abducted, and you're suspect Number One."

"I don't know what you're talking about." Hewston shot Sal a look of pure hatred. "I had a good thing going. I wasn't hurting anyone. Those people I embezzled from have so much money that they didn't even know there was any missing. Then you and that Goody Two-shoes Hammond had to go snooping around. I wish those guys really had hurt her."

That did it. Sal clamped a big hand on Hewston's shoulder and squeezed. Hard. When a waiter started to intervene, Sal sent him a back-off look that had the man scurrying in the opposite direction.

Sal stood and, with his hand still wrapped around the Egyptian cotton of the man's shirt, propelled him out of the bar. "We've got a date with the Savannah PD. Hope you packed your toothbrush because you won't be going home anytime soon."

Olivia knew Sal was investigating the people in her office. She told herself she was prepared for whatever he discovered.

She was wrong.

"You found something?" she asked when he showed up at the office at the close of the work day. She got to her feet, bracing her hands on the edge of her desk.

His nod held no triumph. "Yeah. Shelley put on her computer hat and dug into Hewston's background."

Olivia held her breath. "What did she find? Is he behind the kidnapping?"

"No evidence of that yet. But the man is up to his eyeballs in debt. Fancy cars. Fancy trips. Seems his wife has an eye for the finer things in life. He probably could have kept things afloat, but he tried to make money the easy way by playing online gaming. When he got in over his head, he started skimming. He's been stealing from the firm and its clients for over three years."

Even though Olivia had never particularly cared for Bryan, she'd never thought he was a thief. "Calvin would have loaned him the money if he'd known."

"This is more than just getting through to the next pay-check."

"How much?" she whispered.

"Two hundred and fifty thousand dollars. And that's just what we've uncovered so far. There's probably more. When someone's in that deep, he just keeps digging himself in deeper."

Olivia sank in the seat. "I never expected that."

"Hewston's gotten pretty good at covering his tracks. He moves the money around. It's like playing musical chairs. When someone looks into an account, he moves money there. Then he moves it back. He keeps shuffling it around so that it looks like all the money's accounted for."

"Always one step ahead."

"You got it. He had to know things were going to catch up to him pretty soon, though." Sal paused. "There's more."

"What?" Her voice was a thread of sound.

"The two men we tangled with last night?" At her nod, he continued, "Turns out Hewston represented one of them on a DUI beef. Got him off on probation. Seems the two of them have kept in touch. Hewston sent those goons after us. He thought we were onto his embezzlement. I'm sorry. I know you didn't want that."

"No. I didn't." She let it sink in. "What's going to happen to him?"

Sal shrugged. "He'll do time. In fact, I'd say it was a given."

She knew how the legal system worked. Hearing it applied to a man she'd thought of as a colleague, if not a friend, was somehow different. Bryan had sent those thugs to scare her and Sal off, maybe worse. The words worked their way through her mind. They refused to register.

"We have to question Bryan, get him to tell us what he knows," she said at last.

"If he's smart, he'll clam up and hire a slick lawyer."

"I can talk with him, convince him to tell us what he knows about Calvin." She paused. "If he's involved."

"You don't think he is?"

"I don't know."

Sal framed her face with his big hands. From his expression, she knew she wasn't going to like what he had to say. "Why don't you go visit Shelley? She's pregnant, big as a house, and could use the company."

She wasn't fooled. "You want me out of the way, right?"

His nod was rueful. "The most important thing I can do right now is find out who's behind this. That's the best way to keep you alive. Until I can do that, I have to stash you some place safe."

"I can't go into hiding. In case you've forgotten, I have a case to try."

"Get a postponement."

She shook away his hands. "I can take care of myself."

"Really? So why'd you call me in the first place?"

"That's not fair."

He shook his head. "You're right. It's not fair. I don't play fair when I'm scared."

"You're scared?" She didn't believe it. Salvatore Santonni was the bravest man she knew.

"What do you think? Someone wants you out of the way. Do you think anything else matters?" He took a long breath. "When I saw that man put his hands on you last night, I nearly went ballistic."

Sal was right. Her exhilaration of last night had faded, and in its place was the stark reality that someone wanted to hurt her. Or worse.

She and Sal were no closer to finding out who had kidnapped Calvin than they had been a day ago. Just as unsettling, the more she was with Sal, the more she remembered how much she enjoyed his company. Even with bad guys following them and not knowing if Calvin was alive, she liked being with him.

With an impatient shake of her head, she reminded herself that she had work. Now wasn't the time to dwell upon how much she was beginning to care about him. Again.

The part of her that yearned warred against the part that needed to protect herself from being hurt. She had given her heart to Sal two years ago and it had ended in disaster. She didn't know if she had the courage to risk it again.

What she needed was a distraction, something to take her mind off Sal. Work would do that. The case was ongoing and didn't stop just because someone had abducted Calvin and was trying to kill her. She doubted the judge would grant a continuance even if Olivia asked for one. Which she wouldn't. The parents deserved justice now.

TEN

For the first time since he'd returned stateside, Sal wasn't certain of his next move. If it had been any other op, he'd have a dozen scenarios lined up. As it was, he couldn't keep his mind off Olivia.

Denying that he cared for her didn't wash. From the time he'd laid eyes on her again, he knew what they'd shared hadn't died. If anything, his feelings were stronger than ever.

Despite her work as an attorney, Olivia remained largely untouched by the seamier side of life. She wanted to believe that people kept their word, that they'd play by the rules simply because that was how she lived her life.

With several tours of duty in the Middle East behind him, Sal knew that life was seldom fair and that people lied whenever it suited their needs.

He'd enlisted with a wide-eyed patriotism and a determination to serve his country to the best of his ability. He hadn't been afraid of dying. No, his greatest fear was that of failing. Failing his unit. Failing his country. Failing himself.

He'd never lost his resolve to serve his country, but the innocence of that young boy he'd been was tarnished forever. Whatever naiveté he'd once possessed had been stripped away after witnessing the cruelties that people committed against others without hesitation.

Sal had never tolerated those who preyed upon those weaker than themselves. It wasn't in his makeup to do so. From the time he'd been a boy, he'd tried to defend those who needed protection from the bullies of the world.

Now Olivia needed him, and once again, he was afraid of failing. Because if he did, it could cost her her life.

Olivia had insisted on returning to the office to get some work done. Sal knew she needed to rest, but he went along with it. While she went through a stack of papers, he contented himself by watching her.

The lamp on her desk cast her in soft light. He took in the line of her cheek, the stubborn set of her jaw. She had a way of biting her lower lip when she was concentrating that made him want to smile.

Olivia was holding on by a thread. Sal knew it, saw it in the trembling of her hands when she picked up a glass of water, heard it in her voice when she occasionally talked to herself about what she was doing.

She had been threatened with a knife, her boss had been kidnapped, she herself had almost been abducted, and then there was last night's attack. The fact that she was still standing said volumes about her strength and faith. When she leaned back in her chair to stretch, Sal came to stand behind her and rub her neck.

"Thanks."

The shrilling of the phone caused him to drop his hands. She put the phone on speaker, allowing him to listen to the caller's part of the conversation.

"It's time, Olivia." The voice was maddeningly calm. "Are you ready to do your part?"

"Yes."

"Then listen carefully." The voice was irritatingly patient, as though the caller was speaking to a slow-witted child. "Your boss's life depends upon you following instructions to the letter. You can do that, can't you? Follow instructions?"

"Of course I can." The snap in her voice had the person at the other end of the line laughing softly.

"Temper, temper. Be careful. You don't want to make me angry. Chantry's desk has a concealed drawer. Inside is a thumb drive. We want it. Bring it to us and we'll turn him loose." The voice gave instructions to meet at a boat slip at the docks. "Leave the drive in a brown paper bag in the blue trash can. It's almost over. Do as you've been told and your boss will be released."

The call ended as abruptly as it had started.

"You know about the drawer?" Sal asked. "How to open it?"

She nodded. "Calvin bought the desk from an antiques dealer who pointed it out. When the desk was delivered, he showed the drawer to me." A faint smile touched her lips. "He was so excited about it, like a little kid with his first bike."

"Let's go get it." They headed to Chantry's office.

In the opulently appointed office, Olivia walked to the desk and kneeled in front of it. She reached beneath and pressed a button. A small drawer, cleverly concealed by intricate carvings, slid open noiselessly. Inside, as the kidnapper had said, was a thumb drive.

"We need to see what's on that."

Back in Olivia's office, Sal inserted the drive in the computer. The documents on the drive revealed that Hewston had been selling information concerning Olivia's plan of attack in the court case to the pharmaceutical company. If he knew that Chantry possessed such proof, no wonder he'd kidnapped the man in an effort to get his hands on the file. He must have been desperate. Sal realized something else as well. That made someone in the company Olivia was fighting as dirty as Hewston.

"Why are they still going through with this?" Olivia wondered aloud. "Why not release Calvin? Bryan's already in jail."

"He's in jail for embezzling and assault. If this gets out, it will send him to prison for a lot longer." Sal hesitated. "This implicates the drug company as well."

"I thought I knew him. It turns out I didn't know him at all."

Olivia tucked the USB drive inside her briefcase. She saw a similar-looking drive there and remembered she still had the "leaf-peeper" pictures she'd taken last fall during a trip to Connecticut. Her goal had been to print the pictures and scrapbook them. Of course, she'd never gotten around to it.

Work had a way of interfering with the rest of life. Once Calvin was safely home and the case against the pharmaceutical company was over, she intended on changing that. Though she loved her job, she wanted a life outside of it.

One that included Sal? She pushed that thought away and concentrated on the present.

"We need to be ready for the exchange." She'd gone over the kidnapper's instructions. She had to carry them out exactly. That was Calvin's best chance. His only chance.

"You really think they're going to hand over your boss just like that?"

Doubts, which she'd deliberately ignored, now assailed her. "That was the agreement."

"You can't be that naïve. Hewston has every reason to make sure Chantry doesn't survive. He may beat the embezzling rap, even his part in the mugging if he has a good enough lawyer. But he won't be able to talk himself out of what your boss knows if he's alive to testify."

Bryan's part in the kidnapping still baffled her. She found herself voicing her doubts aloud. "Bryan's weak. He doesn't like to get his hands dirty. Everything about the kidnapping is ugly. That's not his style."

"That's why he hired thugs to do the dirty work." Sal's

gaze bored into hers. "I'm hoping everything goes according to plan, but they won't have any reason to release your boss once they have the drive."

"Everything will be fine. We just have to do what the kidnappers say." Even as she said the words, she heard the foolish hope behind them. She refused to take them back. She needed that hope, held on to it as she would a lifeline. It was all she had.

"Something's off about this whole exchange. Think about it. Why ask for a drive with the files when they had to figure you'd copy it?"

She'd asked herself the same question and hadn't been able to come up with an answer. Then or now. The kidnappers had to know that files could be copied with a press of a computer key. In fact, she and Sal had done that last night after looking at what the drive contained.

Nothing added up, including Bryan's part in the plot. "What about the men who attacked me in the office and then tried to kidnap me? How do they fit in?"

"At a guess, more of Hewston's hired muscle." The hard glitter in Sal's eyes warned her that she wasn't going to like what he'd say next. "I know Chantry has been more friend than boss—"

"He's family."

Sal continued as if she hadn't interrupted. "But you need to be prepared that this isn't going to go down the way you want."

"Why do you keep doing that?" Anger spilled over and out. "Doing what?"

"Making me fear the worst." Didn't he know how much she needed to hope, to believe that everything would be all right?

"Because I'm trying to keep you alive."

ELEVEN

They didn't speak on the way to the docks. Olivia sat in tight-lipped silence, hands clenched in her lap, refusing to look at him. Sal understood her anger. He'd taken away her hope, her belief that they would get Chantry back safely.

Though Sal regretted hurting her that way, she needed to prepare for the worst. Once abductors had what they wanted, they most often got rid of the hostages. That was the only ending that made sense to them.

At the dock, he parked the truck and rounded it to help Olivia out. She wrinkled her nose. He didn't blame her. Brine and diesel oil brewed together in an unpleasant mix. Longshoremen worked at unloading freighters. Shouts pierced the air.

She nodded her thanks but still didn't say anything to him. Finally, she touched his arm. "I'm sorry. You were only trying to help if…if things don't go the way we want."

"You don't have to do this," he said. "I can put the drive in the trash can."

"They told me to do it. I have to do this. For Calvin."

Sal didn't answer but pointed to the can the kidnappers had designated. Per instructions, Olivia set the bag containing the drive in it.

"It's done. Calvin will show up any moment. You'll see." He wished he felt as confident.

"What are they waiting for? We gave them the drive."

Sal knew she didn't expect an answer.

A man appeared on the bow of a boat. Judging from Olivia's cry of joy, it was Chantry. She waved and he raised his arm in return.

"Calvin! Calvin!" She started to rush forward, only to be stopped when Sal clamped an arm around her waist.

That suddenly, the boat was engulfed in flames. Black smoke belched from it. Murderous reds, violent oranges lit the sky. The smell hit them in the face. Bitter. Acrid. The stench reeked of destruction. And death.

Sal pushed Olivia down, fell on top of her.

The earth trembled. He curved his body over her, protecting her from the raining debris of metal and wood.

"Open your mouth!"

"What?"

"Just open it." Keeping their mouths open would prevent their eardrums from rupturing.

"Are you okay?" he asked when the explosion had subsided.

"I th-think so. What about you?"

"Fine. Let's get you out of here." He stood, held out his hand to help her up. "Can you stand?"

"I have to go to Calvin. Maybe he's hurt and needs help."

"You can't help him. Not now."

"We have to do something." She struggled against Sal's hold on her, but she was no match for his strength.

Sal turned her around, pressed her against his chest. "You don't need to see this."

"Too late. I already have. I saw my friend being burned alive."

"We need to get the USB back."

Olivia nodded, unable to do anything more. But when Sal went for the USB, gunshots rang out.

The shots weren't coming from the where the boat had been docked only minutes ago but from a different direction. Sal grabbed Olivia. They zigzagged across the dock and ran toward his truck.

He yanked open the door, and she climbed inside. They didn't wait for the police to show up but sped to the police station. At the police station, they headed to Detective Nynan's office.

The detective stood. "You two again? What have you gotten yourselves into this time?"

Sal gave a terse account of what had happened. "We didn't feel like sticking around for the police to show up."

Nynan picked up his phone, barked out a couple of orders, listened, then nodded. "Let me know what you find." He turned back to Olivia and Sal. "Officers have already responded. I have some questions for you folks."

Before Olivia could respond, Sal said, "Ms. Hammond has had a shock. I'll answer any questions."

She pulled herself up. "I can answer questions."

He gave her a probing look. "Are you sure you're up to it?"

"I'll have to answer them sometime. It might as well be now."

The warm approval in his eyes wrapped around her heart. "We stay as long as you're able. Then I'm taking you home. Shock is going to set in."

"I'm not in shock," she protested.

"You will be," he predicted. "Right now, you're feeling numb. That's good. It lets you keep functioning. But that won't last forever. And then you're going to crash."

He was right. She would have thought of it for herself, but the numbness he'd spoken of was causing her thought processes to turn sluggish.

"Let's do it. Before I change my mind."

* * *

The police questioning wasn't as bad as Sal had feared.

Nynan took them through the phone call from the kidnappers, finding the drive in the hidden drawer and then putting it in the trash can. His eyes narrowed when Olivia confessed to not calling the police immediately after receiving the call. "We could have helped."

"We were trying to save a life," she said.

He nodded curtly. "You say you saw your friend on the deck of the boat and then the explosion happened."

"That's right," Olivia agreed, weariness heavy in her voice.

"We do have something," Sal said and produced the copy of the drive that he and Olivia had made. "You'll find a file about Bryan Hewston. It's pretty self-explanatory."

"Thanks." Another curt nod. "At least you had the foresight to copy it so the evidence isn't gone."

"I think we've gone over everything," Sal said. "And now, I'm taking Olivia home."

The last days had caught up with her. The smudges of exhaustion beneath her eyes had darkened with every hour.

He wanted to erase the shadows, to wipe away the fear and ugliness that had invaded her life. The impossibility of that caused his mouth to tighten. He didn't like feeling powerless.

The detective stood. "If you think of anything else," he said, "anything at all that will help us catch the people who did this, call me. Anytime." He handed a card to Sal.

Olivia, a lady to her core, said, "Thank you, Detective."

"Thank you for coming in. I know it couldn't have been easy."

"No. It wasn't. But it had to be done. I owed it to Calvin."

"Our forensics team will go over the boat, or what's left of it. We'll find out what caused the fire, trace what accelerant was used. That may give us a lead. Arsonists usually have a signature. We've got a database of local arsonists and explosive experts."

Sal had been interviewed first, then remained quiet while the detective questioned Olivia. Though she'd held up well, she now looked fragile enough to break. He stood, placed a palm under her elbow and helped her to her feet.

Outside, he settled his hand at the small of her back, the proprietary gesture for his sake as much as hers. He was gratified to see that the trembling of her shoulders had subsided and that a bit of color had returned to her face.

What he hadn't reconciled was his own overwhelming need to hold her to him and never let her go. He was here on a job, he reminded himself. Acting on his feelings for Olivia wasn't in that job description.

Sal noticed she was leaning heavily on him. She probably wasn't even aware of it. Without realizing it, he was practically running in his need to get her home, dragging Olivia along with him.

"Sal." The word came out on a pant as she struggled to keep up.

"Sorry." He slowed his pace.

Sal bundled her into the truck, slid into the driver's side and drove to her place. Once they'd reached her townhome, he lifted her into his arms, carried her to the front porch and juggled to find her keys in her briefcase. Inside, he laid her on the sofa.

He then set about making her a cup of tea. He wished he knew how to offer comfort, but he had no words. She'd watched her boss, her mentor, her friend die in front of her and he didn't know the right words to say, the right things to do.

"Sorry. I'm not much good with the 'tea-and-sympathy' thing."

"You're plenty good. Sit. And maybe…"

"What?" he prompted.

"Maybe you could hold me," she said in a small voice. That he could do.

TWELVE

Olivia awoke with a start. She must have fallen asleep. She shifted positions in an attempt to get up and shook her head, trying to dislodge the picture of Calvin dying in the explosion.

She couldn't wipe the image of the burning boat from her mind. She doubted she'd ever be able to banish it. If only they'd arrived a few minutes earlier, maybe they could have saved Calvin.

The memory of him raising his arm to her only to be consumed by the flames would forever be seared into her brain. Smells—acrid smoke, the briny scent of the water, the stink of her own fear—had burned into her memory. Hadn't she read somewhere that smell was the most powerful of the senses?

"Sal?" She looked about, found him in a chair, his vigilant pose making her wonder if he'd watched over her all the while as she slept.

"It's all right. I'm here."

"What time is it?"

"Six."

"In the evening?" She'd slept for more than eight hours. "Why didn't you wake me?"

"You were exhausted. You snore."

"Do not."

He chuckled. "Have it your way."

Memories of Calvin and her father crowded her mind. Without her volition, tears leaked from her eyes. She swiped at them with an impatient hand.

"Daddy and Calvin started the firm in a storefront. They shared a desk. It was a shoestring operation, but they kept at it. Daddy promised himself that he'd never turn away someone who needed his help."

"He sounds like a pretty special man."

"He was." She realized she was grieving not just for Calvin but for her father as well.

Not for the first time, she thought of how grateful she was for Sal's presence. He'd offered her comfort, given her answers and helped her remember that life went on, burning away the raw edges of her grief.

Sal caught her hand in his.

"Calvin's dead." If she said the words often enough, she might begin to believe them. With a start, she realized that she hadn't given Walter a single thought. "I need to call Walter, tell him what happened."

"The police will have already made the notification."

"I should at least call him, see if he needs anything." She found her phone, punched in Walter's number. When the phone rang and rang without any answer, she reluctantly hung up. "He probably doesn't want to talk with anyone right now." She understood. The son's grief had to be far greater than her own.

Tears stung her eyes once more as the magnitude of her loss hit her. It had been Calvin who had comforted her when her father died. It had been Calvin who had mentored her on her first big trial case. He had been a part of her life for as long as she could remember.

And now he was gone.

She'd lost not only her boss but her friend, the man who'd stood as a surrogate parent. "Thank you."

Surprise flickered across Sal's face. "For what?"

"For being here. Tell me what our next step is."

She thought she saw admiration in his gaze.

"You're pretty great. Did you know that?"

She realized how much she had come to depend on Sal. He had protected her with his own body during the explosion, taking care of her when she needed him most, and he was still taking care of her.

But she couldn't continue leaning on him. That wasn't who she was. She took care of herself and, with the Lord's help, handled whatever life threw her way. That was rule number one in her book.

Tears stung her eyes, but she refused to give in to them. Tears wouldn't bring Calvin back. Nor would they solve his murder.

So she steadfastly held them back and focused on what Sal was saying.

"This is more than getting back some files," he said.

Once more she had to concede that he was right. Just as with Bryan, she hadn't known Calvin as well as she'd thought she had. What secrets had he harbored? Why hadn't he shared them with her? It reminded her that two years ago she'd believed she knew Sal, but she'd been wrong since he'd been able to leave her so easily.

"We can't leave it this way."

"No," Sal agreed. "We can't."

It had been a horrific day. There was no getting around it. But knowing that he was there eased some of the heartache.

Her growing feelings for Sal created more than a bit of confusion in her. Two years ago, they'd parted. Now he was back in her life and she realized that she wanted him to stay right there.

* * *

Sal thought about what had just passed between him and Olivia.

There'd been a connection. He wanted that. More than he should. He'd promised himself that he'd keep it all business.

Nothing had changed from two years ago when he'd walked away. He was still the Hawk. Still the man who had spotted enemy combatants for a sniper to take out. If the sniper had been unable to perform his duty for whatever reason, Sal had taken over.

If he let himself, he could still picture the deadly M4 carbine, feel his shoulder supporting the weight of the stock, remember the scent it left in its wake.

Olivia came to stand beside him, laid her hand on his arm. "What is it, Sal? What's filling your eyes with such sorrow?"

How did he answer? "It's nothing that you need to worry about." He hadn't meant his words to be a rebuff, but apparently she took them as that for she removed her hand. "I'm sorry. I didn't mean…" Of course he'd meant to shut down her questions. "I'm sorry," he repeated.

What would Olivia think if he told her about his past? She'd recoil in disgust. Her world was filled with light and truth and love. His was shrouded in darkness. Not even Jake Rabb, a Delta buddy, knew of Sal's missions while he'd been in Afghanistan. His orders were buried so deep that only those possessing the highest security clearance knew of them.

Sal knew his friends from Delta wouldn't judge him— they risked their lives every day—but he judged himself. Something had changed inside of him. The man who had gone to war, determined to serve his country, had become a man who abhorred violence. That his current job

demanded he use violence upon occasion didn't alter his
distaste for it.

Accepting that shift was one of the hardest things he'd
ever done. Sometimes he wanted to return to that simpler
time, when he understood what he was doing and why he
was doing it. Now that understanding had become blurred.

He knew he had to make peace with his past. For his
sake. For his family. And maybe, just maybe, for Olivia.

His thoughts circled back to his family. They knew he
had been Delta. His father, a big, bluff man, couldn't have
been prouder. His mother had turned to her faith during
those years, always praying for her son's safe return. But
neither knew of his special assignments.

What would they think if they knew the truth—that
he'd been a spotter for a sniper, giving the go-ahead for
enemy targets to be taken out? Would they be repelled by
the knowledge or would they understand that he'd been
doing his job?

And what of Olivia? What would she think? He backed
away from that. He didn't want to know.

"Where did you go?" Olivia asked when the silence
turned as thick as the humidity.

"Took a trip to the past."

"Must not have been a pleasant journey."

"Why do you say that?"

"Your face. It looked like you were in pain."

"Maybe I was." He didn't elaborate, and Olivia refrained
from asking further questions.

When the judge presiding over Olivia's case learned of
Calvin's death, he granted a continuance, giving Olivia a
much-needed break. She was still reeling and needed time
to grieve and work on other things. The firm had other
cases that required attention.

Sal took her to the office, hovering like a mother hen until she asked him to go out and pick up some lunch.

A call from the police informing her that Bryan wanted to see her came as a surprise. She was going to refuse, but then thought better of it. His actions had caused the death of a good man. She wanted to confront him, to hear him admit his guilt.

When Sal returned, she told him of Bryan's request.

"You don't have to go."

"I do."

They made the trip to the police station, the fourth in as many days.

A sergeant showed them to the room where Bryan waited, his wrists shackled together, the chain bolted to the table. In prison orange, he looked pale, defeated and not at all like the arrogant man she had worked with for the last several years.

"You wanted to see me?" She and Sal took seats in the metal chairs across the table from him.

Bryan lifted his head and shifted his gaze to Sal. The despair in his eyes was belied by his first words. "What's *he* doing here?"

"He's here because I asked him to be here. If you've got a problem with that, we're done."

"No," he said quickly. "No problem."

"Why did you want to see me?"

"They're charging me with murder. You know me, Livvie. You know I couldn't kill anyone. I didn't have anything to do with Chantry being kidnapped. Or killed. You've got to believe me." Bryan's voice held the rough edge of someone who was terrified.

Her lips compressed at his use of her nickname. "Why should I believe you? You sent those men after us."

"Yeah. I did." His voice held not a hint of apology. "You

brought it on yourselves, digging into my life. You had no business doing that."

"You made it my business when you embezzled from the firm and when you kidnapped Calvin." She pushed away from the table and made to get to her feet.

"Don't go. I'm sorry. I copped to the embezzling, sure, but I had nothing to do with kidnapping our illustrious leader or murdering him." The sarcastic words took on a note of desperation, those of a supplicant who knew he'd done wrong but was still begging for mercy. "Seriously. You've got to believe me," he repeated. "I admit to doing some stupid stuff, but no way would I kidnap someone, much less kill him."

"What about hiring someone to do it for you just like you hired those thugs?" Sal countered.

Bryan withered under Sal's hard glare. He looked like what he was, a pitiful human being who excused his failings by blaming them on others. The gloss that had once coated him had peeled away like a cheap veneer.

Despite her contempt for Bryan, Olivia found herself believing him. True, the evidence pointed to him, she argued with herself, and he had confessed to several crimes that would send him to prison for a number of years and have him disbarred, but he'd steadfastly denied being involved in Calvin's abduction and death.

"You know me. Know I couldn't kill anyone. I need your help. Please," Bryan implored. "Convince the police that I didn't have anything to do with Chantry's death."

"What about the file Calvin had on you?" Olivia asked.

"What file?" he demanded hotly and tried to stand despite the chains bolting him to the table. "You're talking like I know what's going on. If there's information saying I had something to do with Chantry's kidnapping and murder, then it was planted."

Olivia heard the shocked vehemence in his voice. It

sounded genuine. "The one showing that you took bribes from someone in the pharmaceutical company."

"That's a crock." Bryan sat back. "You've got to help me. Someone is framing me."

Without making any promises, Olivia and Sal left.

"You believe him, don't you?" Sal asked as they walked out of the police station.

"I think I do," she said, shading her eyes against the blindingly white light of the sun. "Bryan's weak, but he's not a murderer. What about you?"

"He's messed up, sure, but he doesn't strike me as the kind of man to do what was done to your boss. He could have hired those thugs," Sal continued, "but you're right, he's basically weak. He embezzled because it was easy. Cutting off Chantry's finger, rigging the boat to explode, those were hard. I don't think Hewston has the guts for either."

"We can do some digging, see if there was someone in the company offering Bryan bribes."

"Good idea. That will either tear his story to shreds or…"

"Prove his innocence," Olivia finished.

Sal was glad to take Olivia out of there. He'd seen the shock and pity move into her eyes when Hewston confessed to what he'd done. He'd freely admitted to sending men after her, men who'd been told to "rough her up," but she'd still managed to find sympathy for him.

It was her faith, Sal thought, that gave her a bedrock of grace for those who didn't deserve it.

He frowned as he noticed the gray sedan two cars behind him. It had tailed them for the last four turns he'd taken. It could be a coincidence.

Or not.

He didn't signal for the next turn, took the corner

abruptly. The sedan did the same. Sal kept an eye on the rearview mirror. He hadn't been mistaken. Someone *was* tailing them.

"We're being followed."

Automatically, Olivia started to look over her shoulder. "Who? How long?"

"Don't look." She stopped midturn. "Gray sedan. For the last few blocks."

"Who is it?"

"That's what we're going to find out." Sal made a sharp turn, cutting across three lanes of traffic.

Angry shouts sounded and horns blared, but he ignored them. He wanted to get behind the car following them.

Another turn and he was now two blocks to the east. He took a hard right, and, within a few minutes, was once more on the street where he'd been, now three car lengths behind the sedan. Sal maintained that distance until he could safely move ahead of the car. With a quick twist of the wheel, he maneuvered the truck at a perpendicular angle to the other vehicle.

Glock raised, he tore out of the truck. "Stay here," he yelled but wasn't surprised to find Olivia close behind him. He pulled open the door to the sedan. "Hands where I can see them."

"I'm going to use my left hand to reach inside my jacket and pull out my creds," the driver said.

Sal already knew what the man was going to show him. Nondescript car. Wraparound sunglasses. Dark suit. Wrinkled white shirt. Narrow tie. It all added up. "Feds."

The single syllable held both resignation and relief. He and Olivia weren't being chased by deranged killers. That was the good news. They were being followed by federal agents. That was the not-so-good news.

"Got it in one." The driver held up his federal ID. "Homeland."

The Department of Homeland Security. The agency trumped all the others in terms of power and authority and generally being a pain-in-the-neck when it came to dealing with other agencies.

Sal had butted heads with the DHS when his unit had been assigned to provide security for a member of the state department in Afghanistan. Though the DHS normally concerned itself with stateside matters, they had a special interest in the traveling dignitary and wanted things done their way. With Homeland, it was their way or the highway.

"Why were you following us?" Olivia demanded.

"That's federal business," the man in the passenger seat said.

"I figure it's our business since you've been tailing us." Sal lowered his weapon.

"What do you know about Calvin Chantry?" the driver asked.

"Typical," Sal said. "Never give a direct answer when you can ask a question instead." Realizing that they were blocking traffic, he gestured to a quiet side street. "Let's take this out of the middle of the road."

Sal and Olivia went back to his truck. He ignored the angry shouts from other drivers and pulled the truck around the corner.

The DHS agents followed and parked behind Sal. The driver climbed out of the car. "Look, we're both on the same side."

Sal hiked a brow. "Is that so?" He didn't bother hiding his skepticism. In his experience, the Feds played by their own rules, not caring if they worked well with others or stepped on their toes.

"Yeah. Chantry disappeared and now he's dead. He had information on a case we're investigating."

Not letting any of what he was thinking show on his face, Sal digested that. Whatever Chantry had been mixed up in, it was bigger than a class action suit against a drug company. He caught Olivia's smothered exclamation and knew she'd reached the same conclusion.

It didn't take a genius to figure out that the DHS didn't care about a lawsuit, no matter how heinous the charges. No, there was something bigger at stake. Much bigger. Like terrorism.

"Let's start again. What's the real reason you were following us? It can't be Chantry because, like you said, he's dead. There's got to be something more."

The driver didn't so much as blink. "That's classified. And don't bother asking again. You'll only get the same answer."

Sal hadn't expected anything different, but the vehemence behind the man's words told him a lot.

Passenger-side guy put in his two cents' worth. "If you know something, you're under obligation to tell us."

"*If* we knew something," Sal repeated parrot-like. "Which we don't." The three words held not a hint of apology.

"You want to play hardball?" the man said. "We can oblige. Haul you in. Sweat you a while. See what shakes loose."

"Do you really want a lawsuit against the federal government?" Olivia asked, sounding every bit the uptown lawyer she was. "We can oblige, as well." Though her words were calm enough, Sal heard the fury behind them. When it came to the government trampling on individual rights, Olivia was a firecracker. He was glad they were on the same side.

Driver-man put his creds back in his pocket, straightened his jacket. "Looks like we have us an old-fashioned standoff."

Sal widened his stance, crossed his arms over his chest. "Looks like."

"You don't want to make an enemy of the DHS. We have long memories."

"No?"

"No. Look, we can help each other out. You hear anything, you let us know."

"And you'll do the same?" Sal let his disbelief show.

"You were Army. Delta, right? You know how things work." The driver climbed back in the car. "We'll be close."

"Thanks for the warning."

The agents drove off.

"Do all government agents attend the same charm school?" Olivia asked.

"Pretty much."

"Too bad the charm part didn't stick."

He grinned, then sobered quickly. "But they got their message across."

"What was it?"

"That we'd better watch our step. Homeland plays for keeps. They have unlimited power and aren't afraid to use it."

She lifted her chin. "They don't scare me."

"It's not them we should be scared of."

"Who?"

"Whoever's making Homeland nervous." Sal had met his share of Homeland agents, worked with a few. They were unshakable. Probably because they had everyone else in the intelligence community backing their play. They were the elephant in the room that no one wanted to mess with.

If the DHS was involved, it meant national security was at stake. And that meant Sal and Olivia had landed themselves in a whole mess of trouble.

THIRTEEN

When Sal had confronted the DHS agents, Olivia had watched as the soldier had taken over. The face, the stance, the posture were unmistakable. Each spoke of a man preparing to do battle. Understanding the soldier meant understanding the man, and she realized that she very much wanted to do that. Understand the man.

She knew he was worried. He didn't have to say it. She heard it in his voice, saw it in the hard glaze that turned his dark eyes even darker.

Once in her office, he shut the door, locked it. "We need to talk." He gestured to the chairs.

Out of habit, she sat behind her desk. "What aren't you telling me?"

"What makes you think I'm holding something back?"

"Your eyes. Whenever you think you need to keep something from me, your eyes go all empty. Like you're afraid they'll give your secret away so you make them go blank."

"You ought to be in intelligence. The boys there could use you."

"Thanks. But you're not answering my question."

"No. I'm not."

"If Homeland's involved, it means this is a lot more than just a kidnapping and a murder. Homeland doesn't bother itself with garden variety stuff. They have a bigger agenda."

In the years following 9/11, the DHS had grown exponentially in scope and size. Olivia had heard more than one lawyer bemoan the erosion of civil rights as the federal government had run roughshod over individual rights with the Patriot Act and other legislation.

The complaints weren't unjustified and, in some cases, had uncovered unconscionable abuses. At the same time, she supported the nation's commitment to protect its citizens.

Neither side appeared eager to compromise. Until and unless they did, things were destined to get worse rather than better. She pushed the ongoing debate from her mind. Right now, she and Sal had to find a way to keep investigating without stepping on Homeland's toes.

Was it only four days ago that she'd received the call about Calvin? It seemed that a lifetime had passed. She'd been riding an emotional roller coaster ever since. Sal's arrival had only added to the turmoil. There was no doubt that his presence was comforting, but it carried its own brand of tension.

Sal folded his arms across his chest, looking every bit the formidable soldier he had been. "We've stumbled into a terrorism plot."

"Calvin wouldn't—"

Sal held up a hand. "I didn't say he was part of it, only that the DHS thinks he was. We need to step back."

"What?"

"You heard me. It's gotten too dangerous. We're talking terrorists here. The kind of people who think nothing of killing someone simply because he believes differently than they do."

"Wait a minute. Let me get this straight. You want us to back off because things have turned dangerous?" That didn't sound right. Not from Sal, who had signed up for multiple tours in the Middle East because he didn't like bullies.

"Not me," he said in an even tone. "You. You're bowing out of the investigation. As of now."

Her shoulders went rigid with outrage. "No way."

Sal took her hands, led her to the sofa, gestured that she should sit.

She did but not without glaring in his direction first.

"This is no longer a simple kidnapping case gone wrong. This is big-time stuff. Why else do you think Homeland was following us?"

"You think I'd cut and run because things have gotten a little hairy? You don't know me. You don't know me at all." Her voice rose with every word.

"I do know you. And that's why I'm asking that you leave this to the authorities."

"And you?"

"And me."

"So you want me out of the way for my own good? Is that it?" Irritation kicked in, as it always did, when someone implied that she wasn't capable of taking care of herself.

"In a manner of speaking."

She stood, tried to speak, found that her breath was caught in her throat, and tried again. "This is personal for me. It's as personal as it gets. Calvin wasn't just my boss. He was my friend. Someone killed him and may want to kill me, and I need to find out who it is."

Sal stood as well, faced her down. "You don't get it, do you? This isn't fun and games anymore. This is the real deal. Your boss was killed and he may not be the last." That held an ominous note which she chose to ignore.

"It was never fun and games for me."

"I didn't mean—" Sal scrubbed a hand over his face. "I

don't want to see you hurt." The words were said gently, but she heard the worry behind them.

"If it were your friend who was murdered, would you quit looking for the people responsible?"

He waited so long to speak that she thought he wasn't going to answer at all. "No."

"Thank you."

"For what?"

"For being honest." Something inside of her softened. "I can't stop. Not now. I owe Calvin that. Tell me you understand."

Sal nodded. "I get it. I figured you'd say that. But I had to try. If something happens to you…"

"It won't. I have you at my side."

His gaze bored into hers. "If we're going to keep doing this, we're going to set some ground rules."

Wary, she nodded. "Like what?"

"You don't go anywhere, and I mean anywhere, without me. I'll do whatever it takes to keep you safe, whether or not you like it."

She chafed at that. "Isn't that a little extreme?" One glance at the fierce look in his eyes had her agreeing. "Okay."

"You don't question anyone without running it past me first."

To alleviate the grim turn the conversation had taken, she was tempted to ask if she were allowed to take a breath without asking him first, but clearly Sal wasn't in the mood for jokes.

"This isn't negotiable."

"No," she said slowly. "I can see that it's not."

"Good."

Was it? She didn't hand over the reins of control to anyone. Ever. But she'd done just that with Sal. Why was that?

She wasn't ready to delve into it. Not now. Maybe later,

when she and Sal had found out who had murdered Calvin. Until then, whatever she felt for Sal had to be put on the back burner.

She stole a glance at his profile. Strong, uncompromising, proud. Any woman who gave her heart to him would have to accept that he was a soldier who gave his all to whatever mission he undertook.

Could he do the same with a woman he loved? She knew her feelings for Sal were growing with every day. She couldn't help remembering how her heart had been broken when he'd left her two years ago and feared it was going to happen again.

Sal wasn't surprised at Olivia's refusal to step back. Her heart would always triumph over her sense of self-preservation when it came to those whom she loved.

No, he hadn't expected Olivia to give up. It wasn't in her nature to walk away. Just as it wasn't in his. That made them two stubborn people.

Stubborn could get you killed. And while he was willing to risk his own life, he wasn't willing to risk Olivia's. He searched his mind for some way for her to participate in the investigation that wouldn't put her in danger. Even as the thought formed, he dismissed it. Olivia would see through the ploy immediately.

Her determination to do the right thing was one of the things he admired about her. At the same time, it frustrated him to no end. He couldn't conduct a proper investigation if he spent all of his time worrying about her.

She was an independent woman, one who didn't give up control easily. He was asking that she do just that. Never mind that it was for her own good. Keeping her safe was his primary objective. A mission, and that's what this was, had only one leader.

"If it makes you feel any better, you're 2IC of this unit," he said.

Her brow wrinkled. "2IC?"

"Second-in-command."

To his surprise, she burst out laughing. "I'm second-in-command in a unit that consists of two people. You must have stretched to come up with that."

He grinned, more in appreciation of her than in any real amusement. "Every unit has a 2IC. It's required."

"That makes it all the better."

"Now that we've gotten that settled, let's talk logistics. Our pals at Homeland said Calvin was mixed up with a terrorist cell."

Her protest was instantaneous. "I don't believe that for a second."

"Okay. I get that. But what if he was mixed up in something and didn't know about it?" Sal was withholding judgment on Chantry's involvement, but he didn't share his misgivings with Olivia. She would never believe her friend was part of a terrorist plot.

"That could be, I guess."

"It would explain the kidnapping. If we're going to prove his innocence, we need to find proof."

Sal sighed inwardly. So much for his attempt to convince Olivia to let him handle things. He was fighting on two battlefields: protecting her and adhering to his resolve to keep things professional.

Don't get involved with the client was S&J's number one rule. A wry smile rimmed his lips as he recalled that his buddy Jake Rabb and boss Shelley Rabb had done exactly that and were now married to those respective clients. Still, the rule was there for a reason.

Too often, emotion clouded logical thought. Sal was the first to admit that he wasn't thinking straight when it came to Olivia. Reflecting on how he felt two years ago, he realized that his feelings for her today were far more intense. How was he supposed to protect her when his heart kept getting in the way?

The answer was to get out of his own way. The irony of the situation wasn't lost on him. He could either do the job or give in to his feelings. A sigh escaped. The job came first. Always.

FOURTEEN

The following morning, Olivia rose early and decided to put in some work. When Sal showed up, she was gratified to find that she'd written two motions to present to the court and drafted a brief.

He handed her a small flower-filled basket.

"Pansies? My favorite. How did you know?" Olivia traced the pattern of one delicate petal, the lavender streaked with deep gold. Pleasure swelled in her heart. At the same time, a bubble of panic fizzed in her belly. How was she going to say goodbye to Sal when the time came?

"I noticed the pillows on your sofa. Big purple pansies. So I took a guess."

A man who brought her pansies because he'd noticed the flowers on her pillows? Everything went soft and gooey inside her, and she forgot the moment of panic.

"Thank you."

His face reddened. "I just thought that after all that's happened you deserved something pretty."

Soft and gooey melted until it was as mushy as the inside of a cream puff. "Do your teammates know what a sweetheart you are?"

Horror filled his eyes. "No. And don't you be saying anything about this to Shelley because she'll tell Caleb and then it'll be all over."

Laughter bubbled out. "Something to hold over you. I love it."

A panicked look crossed his face. "I mean it, Olivia. I'll never be able to live it down."

"Okay. I mean, I wouldn't want you to lose your reputation as a tough guy. Even though you're really a marshmallow."

"Enough," he said on a mock growl. "Do you want them or not?"

"Yes, I want them. And thank you very much. You were right. I needed something pretty." The last few days had been ugly.

Sal tucked a stray strand of hair behind her ear. "They don't hold a candle to you."

She didn't know how to respond to that. Didn't know how to respond to him. Her heart stuttered, a quick beat of panicked wings. She barely stopped herself from placing her hand there to calm the racing pulse of it. When he looked at her with such undisguised warmth, she felt as awkward as a schoolgirl.

But she wasn't a schoolgirl. She was a woman filled with a bunch of untidy feelings that she didn't know what to do with.

All traces of humor had vanished from Sal's face. If she hadn't known better, she'd say he looked guilty, but he had nothing to be guilty over. Come to think of it, he had been acting strangely ever since yesterday. When she'd questioned him about what was bothering him, he'd brushed her off.

Enough.

"Okay, tough guy. Something's been eating at you. Spill it."

He didn't pretend he didn't know what she meant. "The timing's off."

"What do you mean, 'off'?"

Sal took his time in answering. "I've been going over what happened before Chantry..."

Taking pity on him, she helped him out. "You mean before he was blown up."

"Yeah. Before the boat exploded."

The change of wording wasn't lost on her.

"In the army, we operate on facts."

Impatient, she nodded. "So?"

"So, we've been making assumptions. We don't know if they're true or not."

"Like what?" What was Sal trying to say? And why did she have the feeling that she wasn't going to like it?

"What did we actually see on the boat?"

She worked to recall the series of events in her mind. Calvin had waved to her. She had started toward him, but, before she had taken more than a step, the boat was engulfed in flames. "We saw Calvin die in an explosion." It hurt to say the words.

"Did we? Think about it. We concluded he died in the fire. That's all. Until the authorities finish their investigation, we don't have anything. We saw him on the boat. Then came the explosion. We didn't actually see him die."

"We couldn't see anything because of the smoke."

"Exactly."

"There was a body." She'd learned that firefighters had pulled a body from the wreckage.

"That's right. A body. There's no proof yet that it's Chantry."

"DNA testing takes time."

He nodded. "Time for a man to slip away unnoticed if he wanted."

"What are you saying? That someone else died in Calvin's place? That doesn't make sense."

"I don't know what I'm saying. Not yet. I'm just asking that you keep an open mind."

"As long as you do the same." Olivia struggled to process what Sal was suggesting. "Are you saying you think Calvin is alive?" Hope shimmered in the question, but there was fear as well. What did it mean if Calvin were alive?

Sal didn't answer her question. At least not directly. "We still have more questions than answers."

"If he's alive, why hasn't he gotten in touch with me? Do the kidnappers still have him? Maybe he's injured." Neither possibility was pleasant.

Sal's expression didn't give anything away. "Like I said, more questions."

"What makes you think Calvin faked his own death? What reason could he possibly have?"

"I don't know. What do you know about his personal life?"

Now it was her turn to avoid answering. Calvin had been unusually secretive lately. That didn't mean anything. He'd always been closemouthed about his life outside the office.

"Whatever you're thinking about him is wrong. Calvin's dead. I won't listen to you talk about him that way."

Sal understood that he'd crossed a line. He tried to apologize, but she wasn't having it. He searched for a diversion and remembered that they were going to check on Hewston's claim that he hadn't been taking bribes.

"We need to follow up on Hewston."

Olivia nodded shortly. "We owe him that much."

They spent the morning looking into Hewston's finances, aided by Shelley. He and Olivia didn't get very far, but two hours later Shelley came through.

"I dug deeper into Hewston. There's nothing in his bank records to show any big sums of money," she said. "On the contrary, it appears that a ton of money is going out with very little coming in other than the embezzling. And right now, we can't be sure whether the money is coming from the embezzling or him taking a bribe."

"Thanks, boss." Sal hung up and turned to Olivia. "This doesn't prove his innocence, but it does confirm at least part of his story."

She nodded, started to say something, then hesitated. "I'm sorry for coming down on you like I did," she said at last. "You didn't know Calvin, didn't know the kind of man he was. I can't expect you to have the same faith in him that I did."

Sal only hoped that faith was justified. A call from Nynan saved Sal from having to respond. "What's up, Detective?"

"We have preliminary findings. I thought you and Ms. Hammond would want to know." A pause. "Can you come down to the station?"

"We'll be there in ten."

Sal filled Olivia in on what Nynan had told him. They met the detective at the police station in the promised ten minutes.

After inviting them to have a seat, Nynan folded his arms across his chest. "We found several teeth in the wreckage. We matched them to records at Mr. Chantry's dentist."

"So that's it?" Sal thought through the implications. "It was Chantry who died in the fire."

"I didn't say that. Only that we found some teeth. I'm not speculating on what that means."

"What aren't you telling us?"

"I'm telling you what we found. You have to draw your own conclusions."

"Detective," Olivia said. "I'm having a hard time understanding. You say you found Mr. Chantry's teeth on the boat. Doesn't that mean he died?"

"There were only a few teeth," he said, appearing to choose his words with care. "In this kind of explosion, we'd expect to find more."

"And the body?" Sal asked.

"Is still being processed by the ME. And that's another thing. The body didn't have any teeth attached. None. It almost looks like the body and teeth were thrown in different directions when the boat exploded. We'll have DNA tests run, of course, but they take time." The detective stood, signaling the end of the meeting.

Olivia and Sal walked back to the truck. "We need a break," he said. "You can afford to take a few hours off."

"A drive in the country?" The hope in Olivia's voice told him he was right. She needed time away from grief and work.

"I don't get it," she said as they headed out of the city. "Why are the police stalling? Of course Calvin is dead."

Sal didn't answer. He was too busy watching the navy SUV that had been following them since they'd left the outskirts of the city.

"We've got company. Don't," he cautioned as she started to turn around. "We'll see how far these bozos are willing to go."

He took a sharp right turn, the SUV on his tail. A series of evasive maneuvers failed to shake whoever was following them. His route took them farther into the country. The road narrowed until it was a thin ribbon of asphalt, scarcely wide enough for two lanes. He heard the engine note harden up, the grinding crunch as the driver switched gears.

Sal saw the stock of a rifle appear at the passenger side window of the sedan. This wasn't Homeland. These were hostiles.

"Get down."

A bullet shattered the driver's side mirror. Too close. He

swerved back and forth. He didn't waste his energy firing back. Shooting at a moving object was much more difficult than television shows and movies made it out to be, and he needed all his concentration to keep the truck on the road.

Out of the corner of his eye, he saw a turnoff, little more than a cow path. He hoped their pursuers would miss the road and speed on by.

When he didn't hear the meaty rumble of the souped-up engine behind them, he took a breath of relief. Too late he saw the metal barrier, obviously put there to keep vehicles out. "Hold on."

He cut the wheel just enough to avoid hitting the barrier, but the truck veered into a mud-filled gully, the engine stalled out. His entire body shuddered with the impact.

"Are we still alive?" Olivia's voice reached him as though from a great distance.

"I don't know." He supposed the voice was his. At the moment, he wasn't sure. He wasn't sure of anything. He tried to turn toward Olivia and immediately regretted it. His shoulder and neck screamed in protest.

"You're bleeding."

He touched his forehead and his hand came away bloody.

"Here." She tore a piece off her shirt. When he made to reach for it, she gently pushed his hand away. "Let me." With infinite gentleness, she placed the strip of cloth against his forehead. "That should help."

"Thanks." The gruffness in his voice belied the feelings her touch stirred within him.

"Do you think the doors work?"

It was a valid question. A crash like they'd taken could very well have bent the frame to the doors, jamming them into place.

Sal pushed against the driver's side door. It refused to budge. Okay. That wasn't going to work. "Try your side."

Olivia pushed her door with the same result. "I'll crawl in the back, try one of the doors there."

She undid her seat belt and climbed over the seat. "Easy peasy." She scrambled out. "C'mon."

With considerably less finesse than Olivia had shown, Sal crawled over the seat and climbed out the door as she had, but not without a great deal of pain. He landed with a thud on the ground, further jarring his shoulder, and couldn't bite back the groan that escaped his lips.

"What is it?" she asked.

"Nothing." He needed time to assess the damage to his shoulder. At the same time, he scanned the surroundings. Recon. Once a Delta, always a Delta.

They had to put a whole lot of distance between them and the men who'd run them off the road. Even now he could hear the trampling of underbrush. Gritting his teeth and leaning on Olivia, Sal forced himself to move. Every step was agony, but he kept going. Quitting was not an option. When he judged they'd traveled far enough and the crackling in the underbrush from the men chasing them had faded, he stopped.

The good news was that there was no sign of their pursuers. The bad news was that he was injured more than he'd let on. He and Olivia needed to get out of these woods before he wasn't able to move at all.

He tried to focus on that, rather than on the growing pain stabbing through his shoulder. He'd sustained enough injuries in his army career to know that it wasn't a simple sprain.

"Sal?" Olivia's voice betrayed the fear she had to be feeling.

He didn't blame her. Their situation was grim.

"My shoulder. I think it's dislocated."

"What do we do?"

"You're going to have to set it."

She backed up. "You're kidding. Right?" The last word held a note of hope. He wished he didn't have to dash it.

He let his expression answer for him. "Take off your boot."

"My boot?"

"Yeah." Sal lay back and propped himself up on his forearms. He hated asking Olivia to do this. He didn't mind the pain for himself; he'd been through worse. But Olivia's tender feelings were bound to take a hit when she learned what she had to do. She'd always possessed a fragile courage, but it was going to be put through a grueling test.

"Okay," she said, having pulled off the ankle boot. "What next?"

"You're going to put your foot in my armpit, then yank on my right arm until you hear a pop. That'll mean the shoulder's back in place."

She looked at him as though he'd told her to shoot him in the head. "I can't."

"Yes, you can."

She knelt beside him. "Isn't there any other way? Like I carry you to the nearest hospital and then perform surgery on you with my nonexistent surgical skills?"

"A sense of humor. That'll help."

"Why?"

"Because I'm probably going to pass out for a few minutes, and you can tell yourself jokes while you wait." He scraped up a laugh. It came out sounding rusty, but it would have to do. "You're Delta-strong, lady. So let's get it done and get out of here before some bear decides he wants an extra dinner."

"Sal. Please." The plea in her voice speared straight to his heat. "I can't do this. I'll hurt you."

"It'll hurt a lot more if you don't do it." He spied a sturdy-looking twig, grabbed it and bit down hard. "Do it," he said, the words garbled as he talked around the piece of wood.

Olivia placed her foot in his armpit, then pulled on his right arm. The last thing Sal heard was the pop of his shoulder before he passed out.

"Sal, wake up." Olivia heard the chatter of her teeth. Was she cold or just plain scared? Probably both.

What if he didn't wake up? She'd done as he'd instructed and yanked on his arm with all her strength, while pushing with her foot against his armpit. The popping sound had come just as he'd predicted.

Her stomach roiled at what she'd done. She was the kid in the 4-H Club who had passed out when the troop had visited a farm and witnessed the birthing of a calf. She pushed that memory from her mind. She had to hold it together. For Sal.

She shook him gently. "Sal. Can you hear me?"

He muttered something unintelligible.

She moved so that she could cradle his head in her lap. "I'm so sorry I hurt you."

He opened his eyes, blinked a couple of times. "You did great." His voice sounded like his mouth was full of marbles, but at least he was coherent.

"Can you move?" She glanced around, her gaze seeking out the deepening shadows.

"Don't know." Beads of sweat formed along his hairline and above his lip as he tried to sit up.

She pushed him back down and was alarmed when he didn't resist. "Not yet. Stay put and let me tend you." Though how she was supposed to do that with no supplies, she had no idea.

"We can't stay here. They'll be back."

"It won't do either of us any good if you pass out again." She made her voice deliberately tart. If she didn't, she feared she'd give in to the fear that was crawling up her throat.

She pulled out her phone and wasn't surprised to discover that she didn't have service. "Guess my cell plan doesn't include coverage in the middle of a forest." Though she tried to keep her tone light, she heard the quiver in the words.

Sal must have heard it as well. "All the more reason for us to get out of here."

He was clearly in no shape to walk. What was it with some men that they couldn't figure out that they weren't invincible? She smoothed the hair back from his forehead.

He pushed her hands away. "We've got to put a whole lot of distance between us and whoever was shooting at us. Those were semiautomatic weapons." He'd carried such a weapon when he'd been in Afghanistan. The bursts of fire, impossibly fast cyclic rate and foot-long muzzle flash made the automatic-semis among the most dangerous.

"But why? Whoever's behind this has the drive now."

"We'll figure it out later. In the meantime, we've got to move."

She helped him to a standing position, then propped a shoulder under his arm.

He looked about. "I figure we're about ten miles from the nearest town."

Ten miles? Sal wasn't in any shape to go ten feet, but nothing would convince him of that.

She gritted her teeth. "Let's go."

At first, he refused to lean on her, but as his strength waned with each step, she found herself taking more and more of his weight. At five feet nine inches, she was no weakling, but Sal was a big man, and she knew she couldn't go much farther.

Apparently he knew it as well. "Stop."

She lowered him to the ground, then sank down beside

him. His breathing was labored, and she wondered if he had a broken rib.

"You need to go," he said, letting out a thin sigh. The weariness behind it alarmed her almost as much as the pallor of his face.

She forced a light note into her voice. "And leave you? No way, soldier boy. You and I are joined at the hip until this is over."

He wasn't fooled and didn't bother pretending that he was. "It won't do us any good if both of us are killed."

"I thought you Deltas had a motto about no man left behind."

"That's different."

"Really?" She made herself as comfortable as possible, hoping Sal would do the same. His color was just short of being pasty. "Explain it to me."

"It just is."

She ignored that and set her teeth. "We're getting out of this together. Deal with it."

"You're as stubborn as a Georgia mule."

"And what would you know about Georgia mules?"

A faint smile touched his lips. "I grew up on a farm. And there's nothing more stubborn than a Southern-bred mule."

She tried to distract him. "I have a hard time picturing you as a farm boy."

But Sal wasn't playing. "You go get help. Bring it back."

"And where will you be while I'm getting this help?"

His lips flattened over his teeth. In pain. Or desperation. She wasn't sure.

"Trying to stay alive."

She glanced at the sky, saw the gathering clouds. "We're in for a storm." A storm meant cold and wet. Sal wasn't in any shape to endure either.

She gritted her teeth and pushed herself up, then bent

to help him to his feet. "C'mon. We've got to find somewhere to get out of the storm."

Sal leaned heavily onto her. "Georgia mule," he murmured.

"I wish we had one right now."

FIFTEEN

Taking as much of Sal's weight as she could, Olivia tramped through the forest, steps dragging. She focused on putting one foot in front of the other.

There.

A cave. Shelter. And possibly a bear. She pushed that image from her mind. Right now, they needed a place to hole up where Sal could rest.

She dredged up any information she knew about bears. They hibernated in the winter. Right? So late spring should be safe enough. Any bears around would be out foraging for food. Unless they were seeking shelter, just as she and Sal were.

She left Sal at the entrance to the cave and went to check it out. When she discovered it was empty, she went back for him. "C'mon," she urged. "You need to rest."

Once they were settled and Sal was as comfortable as she could make him, she dumped out her briefcase, looking for the granola bars she routinely stashed there. She saw a flash drive, the one holding her pictures of her time in Vermont. Something was off. She looked more closely and realized that it wasn't the leaf-peeper drive as she'd thought but the one she'd taken from Calvin's drawer.

"I mixed up the drives," she said, explaining what had happened. "That's why those men are after us, isn't it?"

"We don't have all the pieces of the puzzle," Sal said. "Until we do, we're operating in the dark. When we get out of here, we need to stash it somewhere."

Even though the police had a copy of the file, she'd feel better if the original were in a safe place.

"I have a safety deposit box at my bank."

"Perfect."

She found the granola bars. After she and Sal devoured the meager meal, she leaned back against the wall of the cave and wondered how she could take his mind off their predicament. There'd be time enough to worry about that later.

Sal solved the matter by tapping the cave wall. "This reminds me of Afghanistan, staying in grape huts."

"What are those?"

"Houses. But they're made of mud with the thickest walls you can imagine. They were great at keeping out the heat and the cold. Of course, if we were trying to find out if a target might be in one, they made it almost impossible to gather intel." He grew silent, apparently lost in memories.

"We could use a grape hut right along now," she said. The temperature inside the cave was significantly cooler than that outside, and she wished she had something more substantial than her summer-weight navy blue suit jacket to ward off the cold.

"Come here."

She nestled against Sal and relished the warmth he gave off.

"Tell me more about your time with Delta. You must have some really great stories."

"There's nothing great about war."

Sal had always been protective of her and had never wanted to bring the ugliness of war into her world. It had been one of the stumbling blocks between them, his reluctance to share all of himself with her.

"I'm sorry. I didn't mean to pry."

"No." He shook his head. "I'm the one who's sorry. I shouldn't have snapped at you. But war is ugly. I know, that's a cliché. But it's true. It's not just the dying—and there was plenty of that—but the things we were asked to do."

"If you want to talk about it, I'm a pretty good listener." With that, she knew that she truly wanted to know what caused the shadows in Sal's eyes, the pain in his voice when he talked about his days with Delta.

What was he holding back? She knew he'd seen his fair share of action. What didn't he want her to know?

Sal would never do anything dishonorable. Of that, she was certain. His honor was deeply ingrained, an integral part of him. She held her breath, sensing Sal was going to share something more than the usual war story, horrific as that was.

"Our unit was under heavy fire and pinned down. I managed to get to the enemy's machine gun and take it out.

"I was hit in the shoulder and must have passed out. When I woke up, I was in an army hospital. The CO was there. He told me I'd be getting a medal." Another shake of his head. "That was the last thing I wanted. We lost three men that day. When I told him how I felt, he said that the medal wasn't for what I did but for living with it."

Olivia wanted to offer comfort, but what could she say? She reached for him, but he pulled back.

"I know. There's nothing to say. In the end, I asked for a different assignment." His laugh was hollow. "That's how I ended up as a spotter."

"A spotter?"

"I identified targets for a sniper. I made certain the conditions were right, wind, etc. At least then I didn't have faces to go with who I was killing. I got the call name of

Hawk." He met her gaze in a hard stare, as though challenging her to condemn him. Waiting for it.

"This is what you didn't want to tell me? Why you walked away two years ago."

"Don't you get it? I all but put targets on the enemy's back so my partner could take them out."

"You were obeying orders."

His laugh turned bitter. "That's what I told myself. Over and over. But in the end, it didn't matter. I couldn't live with myself anymore. So I got out. While I still had part of my soul left."

Her heart bled for him, a man who had given everything to his country until he had nothing left. His sense of honor and duty had warred with each other, taking chunks of his soul as casualties in the battle.

She'd thought she knew him, but she'd been wrong. These parts of him that doubted his worth, his heart, his honor, those were new to her. They added layers and vulnerabilities and made him more attractive than ever. She was having a difficult enough time resisting his appeal as it was.

What must it take for a man as strong and courageous as Sal to question himself? What another man might pass off as the necessities of war had carved scars in his soul. Though invisible to the naked eye, those scars ran deep.

"I wish you'd told me this two years ago."

His nod was part acceptance, part pain. "Maybe I should have. I don't know." He looked down at his hands, turned them over as though they held the answers he was seeking. "I haven't told my parents. That's why I stay in Atlanta. I don't want to see the disappointment in their eyes if they find out what I've done. What I was."

"Your parents would never stop loving you." Two years ago, Sal had told her about his family and how much they loved each other.

"When I enlisted, I thought I knew everything. Turns out that I didn't know anything at all. And now…" He shook his head.

She took his hand, trying to tell him what was in her heart through touch because she didn't have the words.

"I would have understood."

"How?" The word came out in a harsh growl, and he yanked his hand away. "How can you understand when I don't?"

"I don't have answers. But I know Someone who does. He understands everything because He endured everything."

Sal's nod was weary as if he'd heard it all before.

"Do you think Christ wants only those who are perfect to come to Him? He wants everyone, including the worst sinners among us. He can heal even them." Her voice broke, and tears stung her eyes. "Sorry about that. Talking about the Savior does that to me."

Sal lifted his head, his penetrating gaze locking with hers. "I know you're trying to help, but right now, I'm not ready to hear how the Lord can heal me. Maybe I'll never be ready." The last was said with such anguish that she felt it clear down to her soul.

How she wished she could share her belief with him. Her faith was such an integral part of her that she couldn't imagine her life without it. When her mother had died, she and her father had turned to each other and to the Lord. Their faith had sustained them then as hers had when he died a few years back.

Clearly, Sal wasn't ready to accept the Lord into his life, and she backed off. She wanted to reach out once more to take his hand and press it to her heart, to promise that she would never turn away this man who had given so much.

Sal looked at himself and saw a man beyond redemption. She looked at him and saw a man who needed love. Hers and the Savior's. Maybe one day she could convince him of that.

Sal woke, disoriented and fuzzy-headed. The worst of the pain had passed. He'd slept fitfully, afraid the dream would come. At times of extreme fatigue or stress, it pulled at him. Last night had been no exception.

The faces were there, the faces of the men who died because of him. Why wouldn't they let him go? He had a drawer full of medals, including a Purple Heart and a Bronze Star. He'd give them all back in a heartbeat if it meant he could erase the nightmares that continued to plague him.

Scrubbing his hands over his jaw, he looked around for Olivia and saw her slumped against the wall. Dirt smudged her face. Her hands were clenched as though to fight off attackers.

A small smile lifted the corners of his lips. She'd done everything and more than he'd asked, had reset his shoulder, kept them moving, and then found shelter so that he could rest and get his strength back. He wanted to tell her what was in his heart but knew he couldn't.

The very last thing Olivia needed was for him to complicate matters by telling her that he'd never forgotten her, never forgotten what they'd shared. She was under enough stress as it was.

Though he hated to wake her, he shook her gently. "Olivia."

She blinked, rubbed her eyes.

"It's time we got out of here."

"Are you all right?" she asked, and he knew she was asking about more than his shoulder.

"Better. A lot better. Thanks to you." He stood with difficulty.

She hurried to her feet to support him. After a moment's hesitation, he accepted her help. "Thanks."

He tested his feet, found that he could walk. Outside the cave, he got his bearings. "Ten miles east, we should find a town."

They covered a few miles, and he discovered he had cell coverage. He called Nicco and gave the coordinates from his GPS-equipped phone.

Nicco showed up, took one look at Sal and gave a low whistle. "You just can't keep out of trouble, can you? First stop is the nearest hospital."

"Correction, first stop is the bank. We've got a *deposit* to make. A very important one."

On the way to the bank, Sal made introductions. Nicco darted questioning looks at Sal, who ignored them. Skilled at picking up on nuances, Nicco probably felt the tension that radiated between his brother and the client.

"If what you've got is so important, why not take it to the police?" Nicco asked.

Sal darted a look at Olivia, asking for her permission for him to confide in his brother. She nodded. They'd already discussed the pros and cons of keeping the drive versus handing it over to the authorities. The police had a duplicate. That should be enough.

Sal provided Nicco with a brief rundown of the case. "They have a copy of it. Plus, I have a feeling we're going to need the original before this is over. When we get things sorted out, we'll give it to the police."

At the bank, Olivia went through the procedure of checking out her safety deposit box and putting the drive inside while Sal stood by her. Their bedraggled appearance caused several brows to rise. But nobody questioned them.

As they returned to the truck, Nicco asked, "*Now* can we take you to the hospital?"

Not long after that, Sal was treated for his injuries and rejected the doctor's suggestion that he stay overnight.

"I need your truck," Sal told Nicco.

"No problem. I'll arrange to have yours towed and repaired."

Sal clapped his brother on the shoulder. "Thanks. I owe you."

Nicco's grin was infectious. "You can be sure that I'll collect." He handed the keys to his truck to Sal and took off.

"What will he do for transportation for himself?" Olivia asked.

"Don't worry about Nicco. He'll find something. He's nothing if not resourceful."

"Where do we go from here?" she asked once they were outside the hospital.

Before he could answer, they were stopped by Agents Timmons and Jeppsen, the Homeland Security men they'd encountered earlier.

Though the agents didn't draw their weapons, they made no secret of the fact that they were armed, letting their suit jackets flap open to reveal they were each carrying a suppressed Elite Dark Sig Sauer P226. The weapon was a favored one in law enforcement, carried by a number of Texas Rangers, as well as those in the Spec Ops community such as Navy SEALs.

Their brusque manner told Sal that they were on the hunt. What it had to do with him and Olivia, he couldn't guess.

"We heard you had a bit of trouble," Jeppsen said.

Olivia lifted her chin. "We were run off the road, shot at and nearly killed. So, yeah, I guess you could call that 'a bit of trouble.'"

Her retort nearly caused Sal to grin, but there was nothing funny about a visit from the DHS. "Why is Homeland so interested in us?" he asked.

"Terrorism." The agent's voice snapped Sal back to the here-and-now.

Terrorism. Sal felt his body respond to the word. His muscles tightened, his stance battle ready. He'd suspected it, but having it confirmed sent his instincts on alert.

"You're saying that Calvin was part of a terrorist cell and you think I'm involved as well?" Olivia was in shock. He heard it in her voice, saw it in the uneven rise and fall of her chest.

"He wasn't in the cell per se," the agent said. "But he knew what was going on. He made some very dangerous people very angry at him. In case you were wondering, these are the kind of people you don't want mad at you."

Sal got what the agent was saying. Chantry had been eliminated. It was as simple and as brutal as that. No matter what the man had done, he hadn't deserved to burn to death.

Olivia, regal even in her filthy clothes, drew herself up. "I don't believe you."

"Believe it. Your friend was fronting for a Russian terrorist cell." Timmons looked from Sal to Olivia, his gaze narrowing as it rested on her. "You're saying that you had no idea of what he was doing?" Skepticism colored his voice and had Sal's hackles rising.

"Of course she didn't." Sal wasn't about to let that go unchallenged.

Olivia flashed him a grateful look. "No," she said, turning her attention to the DHS agent. "I didn't."

"We've been following Chantry for months. We knew he was dirty, but we didn't have the goods on him. Now he's dead, and the connection to the people he was fronting is gone." Disgust was plain on his face. Disgust and suspicion.

Though Sal knew that Olivia didn't have anything to do with Chantry's possible treason, he could understand—almost—why the agents were not inclined to believe her. She'd made no secret of her longtime friendship with Chantry or her affection for him. To Sal's mind, that made her appear even more innocent, but not so to the DHS agents.

"That's regrettable but certainly not my fault," Olivia said with dignity.

Timmons flushed an ugly shade of red.

Sal wanted to applaud Olivia for her grace under fire. Timmons had all but accused her of being part of Chantry's plan, and she'd firmly denied the implication.

"Maybe if you'd told us what was going on, we'd have been able to help you," Sal said in a we're-not-going-to-take-the-blame-for-your-screwup voice.

"It was classified, but—"

"That's always the way with you Homeland boys, isn't it?" Sal cut in. "Everything's classified, and you're so afraid of sharing what you know with someone else that you're chasing your own tails."

"People higher up the food chain than us have since given the go-ahead to share limited parts with you," Timmons continued as though he hadn't been interrupted.

Sal thought about telling them about the USB drive but was reluctant to do so. The DHS agents had accused Olivia of plotting against the United States. How did he know they weren't part of the plot and looking to divert suspicion onto someone else?

"When did you catch on to Chantry's part in all this?" he asked instead.

"We've had him on our radar for the last year. Things heated up when he went missing."

"You mean when he was kidnapped," Olivia snapped.

Timmons gave her a long look. "Mighty convenient

for Chantry to disappear just when we were getting ready to close in."

"That's not proof of anything."

"What we're wondering, Ms. Hammond, is how you could not know what your boss and friend was involved in," the agent said, a scowl digging into his mocha-colored skin. "Doesn't seem likely, considering how close you say the two of you were."

"We told you." Sal cut off the agent's line of questioning. "Olivia had no knowledge of what Chantry was up to. If he was a part of some plot, he fooled her like he did everyone else."

"So you say."

"That's right. So I say." Sal let the words hang in the air. He didn't bother prettying them up. Timmons and his partner might as well know from the get-go where he stood: squarely on Olivia's side.

The considering look in the agent's eyes told Sal that the message was received and understood.

"If you think of anything that can help us, we expect to hear from you," Jeppsen said. He and his partner stalked away. Halfway to his car, he stopped, turned. "You haven't heard the last of this."

When the agents had driven away, Olivia looked at Sal. "Thanks for sticking up for me."

"You were doing a pretty good job of it yourself."

"Yeah, well, lawyers learn to develop a thick skin or they don't make it." She grimaced. "Can you believe them? Accusing me and Calvin of being a part of some plot?"

"Homeland doesn't like looking bad. It's not good for the image. They're going to keep coming at us. They need answers, and right now we're the only game in town."

"What they said about Russians made me think about the men who attacked me that first night. I think their accent was Russian."

"That explains a lot. They were probably the ones who tried to take you outside the courthouse, as well."

"And run us off the road yesterday."

Olivia didn't need Sal to tell her that having Russian agents after them raised the stakes. The Russians had a well-earned reputation of playing rough. Automatically, her hand moved to her cheekbone where a tiny scab remained from the knife prick.

The following day, Timmons and his partner Jeppsen showed up at Olivia's townhome with a search warrant.

"This allows us to look anywhere we want," Jeppsen said.

"Can I see it?" she asked, thinking that Sal hadn't been joking about Homeland not leaving them alone. She'd known this was coming and had braced herself for it.

She perused the paper, looking for anything, anything at all, that was out of order. Even a mistake in the address or the spelling of her name could invalidate the warrant. "Okay. I guess it's too much to ask that you clean up after yourselves." She'd witnessed searches at clients' homes and had been appalled at the mess the police had made.

"You're right," Jeppsen said. "It's too much to ask."

The two agents turned the townhouse upside down, unmindful of the shambles they left in their wake.

Three hours later, Timmons said, "Nothing."

"Which I could have told you if you'd asked," she said with no small degree of asperity.

"We like to see for ourselves." Timmons fisted his hands on his hips. "Look, Ms. Hammond. We're in a fix. Chantry and whoever he was mixed up with were planning something big. We're grabbing at straws, trying to figure out what it was. Before it's too late."

"You gotta admit that it looks fishy that you don't know

anything about this, you being so close to Chantry and all," Jeppsen said.

Olivia could almost tolerate Timmons, but his partner was another matter. The man seemed determined to make her the villain of the piece or, at the very least, an accomplice in Calvin's plan.

"Then pay attention," she said, enunciating each syllable with precision. "I am not part of this. I never was. I never would be. So save yourself some energy and find out who else was in on this. It wasn't me."

Timmons shrugged while his partner made no attempt to mask his disbelief.

"You'll be seeing us again," Timmons said.

"Count on it," Jeppsen added.

The two agents took off.

Olivia gave a sigh of relief when Sal arrived to pick her up. She sank back into the truck with a defeated air. She had tons of work to catch up on, especially after spending so much time searching for Calvin, and now she was a suspect.

She wanted to laugh hysterically at the idea that the federal government actually considered her a part of a terrorist cell. Who would they pounce on next? Homeland wielded a tremendous amount of power. No one dared buck them. To do so was to ask for a boatload of trouble.

She worked through what was left of the day. Sal stayed close by, and she was more grateful than ever for his quiet but solid presence. The last few days, which included losing Calvin, being chased by bad guys, spending a night in a cave, and having the DHS accuse both Calvin and herself of terrorism, were catching up to her.

Sal frowned when a text came in just as they were preparing to leave for the day.

"What is it?" Olivia asked.

"Timmons. He wants to meet us at the Sand Dollar

Motel. Room 242. Says he has something we need to see. Twenty minutes." Sal checked his watch. "We need to get moving."

They drove to the seedy-looking motel in the wrong part of town.

"Why meet here?" Olivia asked, nose wrinkling in distaste.

"Your guess is as good as mine." Sal didn't look happy at the setting either.

They tried the door, found it unlocked. He motioned for her to step back and went in first, checked it out. "Looks okay," he said and gestured for her to go inside, closing the door behind them.

The next moment, it pushed open again, and a portly figure entered.

SIXTEEN

"Calvin." Olivia gasped. "You're alive." She struggled to wrap her mind around that as well as the fact that he pointed a gun at her and Sal.

"Very much alive." He held up his right hand. "Minus one finger. It hurt like the dickens, but it had to be done if I was going to sell the whole kidnapping story."

"You cut off your own finger?"

"Had to make it convincing. I knew you'd recognize the ring."

Comprehension settled in. "You bought the ring so I could identify the finger as belonging to you." How long had he been planning this? She thought of something else. "Your teeth were found on the boat."

"I went to an out-of-town dentist, had a few teeth pulled, made sure they'd be found in the wreckage."

"And the phone calls? You made them."

"Give the lady an A. I bought one of those nifty voice synthesizers. I could barely keep from laughing when I called you. You sounded petrified."

She didn't bother hiding her disgust.

"How did you always know where I was?" That was something that had troubled her from the beginning.

"I put a tracker in your briefcase a while back," Calvin said. "You never go anywhere without that piece of junk. I figured a tracker might come in handy someday. Turns out I was right. Then there was the bug in your office. It was almost too easy. I tucked it behind that ridiculous painting."

"Whose body was that in the explosion?" Sal asked.

"Some stiff I bought online. Turns out you can buy just about anything on the net if you know where to look. Including a dead body. Of course, I had to cut off the finger. By the time the DNA results got in, I'd be long gone. Or I was supposed to be."

"How did you know about Timmons and Jeppsen?"

"Those two bozos have been following me for the better part of the year. Why do you think I had to disappear? It was child's play to spoof Timmons's phone and get you here."

His words were a slap in the face, wiping away everything she thought she knew about the man she'd called friend. "I don't know who you are." Grief coated each syllable. She thought of all the pain his actions had caused. "I was almost killed because of you. And Bryan, you set him up. He was never a part of this." Her instincts had been correct, but she'd never suspected Calvin of being behind the plot to pin the kidnapping and murder on Bryan. How could she have been so wrong about him?

"Of course I set him up. He was a patsy waiting to be used. I've known about his embezzlement from the first. I bided my time, waiting for the right moment to use it. The little twerp stole from me. *Me*. He got what he deserved. I put that file about him selling secrets on the drive as insurance. If anyone found it, they'd concentrate on that, wouldn't look further.

"I knew Homeland was on my tail and that they were closing in. In my hurry to get away, I forgot the drive. Still, everything would have been all right if you had brought the right drive to the exchange." Accusation rang loud in his voice.

"Why didn't you just call me, ask me to bring you the drive?" Olivia asked. "Why all this cloak-and-dagger?"

"I'd originally planned to ask for money for ransom, but after leaving the drive, I thought it would be the perfect thing, not to mention throwing blame on Hewston and the drug company."

Calvin made a rude sound and directed all his venom at Olivia. "How could you have been so stupid as to mix up the drives in the first place? You think I wanted a drive with pictures of leaves on it?" He nearly spat the last.

What was she supposed to say? *I'm sorry I interfered with your terrorist plot?* She knew a wild desire to laugh at the absurdity of it. She shook her head in bewilderment. "I don't understand. Any of it."

"Let's just say I happen to be really fond of the color green." He gave a lipless smile that was somehow worse than no smile at all.

And then she got it. It had been obvious, if she'd been looking. Calvin's extravagant lifestyle. His insistence upon having the best of everything. "Money."

"You're catching on." As he sneered, he didn't look anything like the man she remembered. "Now, if you'll excuse me, I have places to go." He grabbed her briefcase. "I figure you still have the drive in your briefcase. Once I have it, I'm home free."

Only the USB drive wasn't in her briefcase. Not any longer.

"Goodbye, Olivia." Calvin clicked something, then darted out the door.

She heard the ticking. "What is that?"

Sal scanned the room, pointed to what appeared to be a small clock sitting on a table near the door. "A timer."

She started for the door, but Sal grabbed her. "The

bomb's rigged to the door." He pushed her toward the bathroom, then grabbed the mattress from the bed, dragged it in after them. "Bathtub," he shouted.

She scrambled inside the tub and lay down.

He did the same, covering both of them with the mattress. "Whatever happens, stay down."

Just as he said the last word, the room exploded. Olivia struggled to breathe beneath Sal's weight and that of the mattress. Indistinct thuds sounded. Probably pieces of drywall landing on them, she thought with the small portion of her brain still functioning.

She registered Sal's chest pressed against her back, his arms protecting her head. She prayed the mattress was shielding him from the worst of the falling debris.

The very air seemed to shake. Or maybe it was her. She couldn't tell. When the aftershocks stopped, she took a shallow breath. Another.

She struggled to get up, but Sal urged her back down. "Not yet."

"Is it over?" she whispered after several minutes had passed.

"I think so."

Sal pushed the mattress off them. He climbed out, then helped her out. When her legs threatened to give way, he clamped his hands on her shoulders and held her against him. "Better?"

"Yes. Thanks."

A chalky substance covered their faces and arms. Dust from exploding drywall, she thought absently. Her mouth was dry, and she wet her lips.

Cautiously, she and Sal picked their way over the rubble in the room and out to the landing.

"Careful where you step," he warned. "We don't know how far the damage goes."

They hurried off the landing and down the stairs. People

were spilling out of doors, bewildered expressions turning to horror when they saw the gaping hole of what had been the motel room. Cell phone cameras were pointed in their direction.

Olivia cringed. The last thing she wanted was for her picture to be trending on social media sites.

Sal kept his arm around her, turned her face toward his side. Another grief-induced breath drew raggedly through her. An unfamiliar sensation in her ear had her putting her hand to it. She wasn't surprised that her finger came away bloody. Though she'd remembered to open her mouth as Sal had told her during the explosion at the dock, her eardrum had probably ruptured this time due to the proximity of the blast.

"Here." Sal handed her his handkerchief. "Your ear should be fine in a little while. In the meantime, keep taking shallow breaths.

"Better get ready for questions," he advised as sirens sounded in the distance. "From the police and the fire investigators."

Olivia took a bracing breath. Answering a bunch of questions from the authorities was the last thing she wanted to do right now, but better to get it over with. When had her life spun so out of control?

He tightened his arm around her. "We'll get through this." The words were simple enough, but, like a quiet smile, they comforted and warmed.

What would she have done if Sal hadn't been here? He'd saved her life. Again. If not for his quick thinking, they would surely have died in the explosion.

"Calvin tried to kill us." Her words were as broken as she felt. Even after knowing that Calvin had deceived her, she couldn't believe that he'd wanted her dead. Had everything she'd ever known about him been a lie?

Her roiling thoughts ripped through her memories,

memories going back more than two decades, churning up every experience and every moment spent in Calvin's company. How had she not seen what he was? How had she been so stupid?

Whatever grief she was feeling was now overshadowed by fury. Fury at Calvin. Fury at herself. Fury that she could be so easily deceived.

This wasn't over. Calvin had to be brought to justice. He had almost gotten away with his plot all because she'd been too blind to see what he truly was. She should have looked beneath the polished exterior to the ugliness that festered inside.

She turned back to stare at the yawning maw of the blown-out room, the desolation a metaphor of her feelings. Both had been destroyed by a man who put greed above all else.

She and Sal were treated by EMTs who offered to take them to the hospital. Both refused. They had work to do.

After the police were finished with them, Sal took Olivia home. She'd excused herself to clean up, reappearing thirty minutes later in a white top and jeans.

Floating on exhaustion, she looked almost ethereal in the soft glow cast by moonlight streaming through the plantation-style shutters. Sal barely refrained from reaching for her. It would be a mistake to touch her when his feelings ran so hard and fast.

He knew he was in danger of stepping over his self-imposed boundaries. If he did, what then? The point of no return loomed close. Too close. He needed to take a step back from Olivia and his growing feelings for her.

He focused on the practical. "You need to eat."

"I'm not hungry."

"You still need to eat." He placed the sandwich he made on a plate and set it on the table.

She picked up the sandwich and took a bite, chewed, swallowed. "You're right. How could I be hungry and not know it?"

"You've been running on fumes for the last week." He hesitated, not wanting to add to her burden, but this could be important. "There's something else that's been nagging me ever since Chantry showed up. He said that if someone found the drive and saw the file about Hewston, they wouldn't be tempted to look further."

Olivia nodded. "That's been bothering me, too."

"We need to get that drive to someone who knows a lot more than I do about computers."

"Like Shelley?"

"Like Shelley. If there's something on there to be found, she'll find it."

They shared a smile. There was no one better at decrypting hidden files than Shelley Judd, and she'd be the first to say so.

With that out of the way, Sal focused on how to help Olivia get through the next hours. He knew her boss's actions had chewed up her heart and then spit it out in little pieces. Her next words proved it.

"I can't help wondering if everything in my life was a lie. Calvin wasn't just my boss. He was my friend. What does it say about me if that's the kind of friends I attract?"

Sal wanted to tell her that it said she looked for the good in everyone, but he knew she didn't want to hear that. She probably didn't want to hear anything except that it was all a big mistake.

Tears pooled in her eyes. He watched the movement of her throat, saw her swallow. It was obvious that the effort cost her. Of course, it did.

She'd just learned that the man she had looked up to, had thought of as an uncle and a mentor, was dirty, dirty right up to the starched collar of his designer shirt and the knot of his silk tie. She had believed in him until she couldn't deny the evidence of his guilt any longer.

Not only was he dirty, he had tried to kill her.

What must that do to her?

Sal wanted to promise to make everything all right, but he was powerless to do that just as he was powerless to take away the pain. With a startled realization, he knew that he wanted to do more than that. He wanted to make a life with her.

He couldn't give that to her, not with his past that cast a shadow over every part of his life, but he could keep her safe. Olivia knew of the darkness within him, but eventually she'd look at him with disgust. He couldn't bear that.

She was holding up, had even found a small smile. "I wanted the truth. Looks like I got it. And then some. Nothing was real, was it?" And the smile, tiny as it was, slid right off her face. "Everything about Calvin was a lie. How could I have been so stupid? I believed him, believed in him."

"None of this is on you."

"Isn't it?" she challenged. "I thought I knew him. Now I'm sure I didn't know him at all. It feels like I don't know anything anymore."

"That's the grief talking."

"There's no grief," she denied, her voice a shadow of its normal resolve. "The man I thought I knew didn't exist. So, no, I'm not grieving over him." The anguish on her face as well as the self-blame in her voice tore at his heart.

"You just said it. The man you thought you knew didn't exist. You're grieving over that."

"I can't get a handle on it. Not any of it." Tears formed in her eyes, the glistening drops clinging to her lashes.

Sal resisted the urge to wipe them away. To touch her now would spell disaster for both of them. If he gave in to the desire to comfort her, he'd be unable to prevent himself from kissing her.

He wanted to spare her the suffering but knew she would have to process it in her own way in her own time. "Give yourself a break. You've been going flat-out for days. No one can keep that up."

And then the dam broke. Sobs shook her slender body. He pulled her to him, her temple pressed against his chest as misery overtook her.

He would have taken the pain for Olivia if it had been possible. Watching her shatter into pain-filled shards twisted his heart, his gut. How would he feel if someone he'd thought of as a friend had done the same?

When she drew back, she wiped her eyes with the sleeve of her shirt.

"I want to say that I know how you're feeling," Sal said, "but I don't."

"But there's Someone who does."

Confused, he stared at her until he realized she was speaking of the Savior.

"Jesus was betrayed by a man He'd made a disciple. I picture Christ asking Himself why a friend turned against Him as Judas had. It must have caused Him unbelievable torment."

As Sal watched, a fierce resolve settled on her face, a resolve born of pure steel. "We have to stop Calvin. We have to make things right."

Sal had never been more proud of her than he was at that moment. She had gone through the refiner's fire and had emerged all the stronger for it.

Olivia gazed at him with tear-wet eyes. "The Lord knows and understands our heartaches, our weaknesses, our fears. Yours and mine and that of everyone else on earth." She thumbed away the remaining tears.

Sal felt tears sting his own eyes. "You sound like you've had personal experience with it."

"When my father died, I fell into depression. It got so bad that I couldn't get out of bed, much less go to work. Finally, I knew I had to do something. I took my grief to the Savior. He didn't take it away, not at first, but He gave me the strength to deal with it."

Emotion wadded up in his throat. Sal cleared his voice with a rough cough, trying to put an end to the subject.

Hurt flickered in her eyes. He'd cut off what had promised to be a deeply spiritual discussion. At one time, he'd been an active believer. His time in Afghanistan had changed that.

What he'd witnessed there had chipped away at his faith until he started questioning what he'd once believed. How could a loving God allow such cruelties to occur? By the end of his last tour of duty, he hadn't been able to reconcile the atrocities he'd seen with the God he thought he knew.

"Talking about faith isn't easy," she said, correctly interpreting his reluctance to continue the conversation. "It's sacred, but the Atonement is the greatest gift the world has ever known. Because of it, the Lord has taken our sins upon Himself." She took his hand. "What I said in the cave—it hasn't changed. He's there for you. You just have to go to Him."

SEVENTEEN

The following morning, Olivia and Sal drove to the bank and retrieved the drive.

"We'll make a copy, give it to Homeland, then I'm going to express the original to Shelley, see what she can make of it," he said.

Olivia nodded, relieved that they weren't holding back on the DHS any longer. She didn't want to get on Homeland's bad side, no matter how obnoxious the agents were. She couldn't forget the chill that had gripped her ever since Jeppsen and Timmons had accused her of being part of a terrorism plot. "What can we do in the meantime?"

"What would you normally be doing on a weekday morning?"

She didn't have to think about it. "I'd be at the office, drafting briefs or preparing motions or going over closing arguments."

"Then that's what you'll do. The best way to get through life's hard stuff is to keep living."

She thought about that and realized Sal was right. She had a job she loved, a job she believed in. Even though the judge had given her a continuance, the case still needed work.

As she'd expected, the office was in turmoil when she arrived, the story of what Calvin had done all over the news. Everyone, from the mail boy to the partners, buzzed around her. Though she wasn't a partner, they looked to her because the Hammond name was on the door.

"What's going to happen, Ms. Hammond?" Julie, the receptionist, asked. "Are we closing down? I can't afford to lose my job."

"Not if I can help it. For now, everyone should just go about business as usual." She spent time with each individual, talking through their disbelief of what Calvin had been mixed up in and the fear of possible unemployment.

Things settled down after that, and she and Sal retreated to her office. Sal's suggestion that he pretend to be a security expert had been a stroke of genius. No one questioned his presence, not after all that had happened, first with Bryan and then with Calvin.

"You were great with them," he said. "You were nearly killed yesterday, but you go to work and take care of the people here."

"They're family," she said simply.

Sal bent his head, his lips hovering a fraction of an inch over hers. She placed her palms against his chest, felt the steady beat of his heart, absorbed his strength.

The shrill of his phone interrupted the fragile moment. Sal took the call, his expression growing darker by the second. "No way," he shouted. "You can't ask that of her."

"Who was it?" Olivia asked when he hung up.

"That was Timmons. Chantry called Homeland. He wants to turn himself in, but he'll do it only to you. It's supposed to go down tonight." Fury whipped through his voice.

"If it means bringing Calvin in, I have to do it. I don't have a choice."

"The DHS uses people. Right now, they want to use you. There's no guarantee for your safety." Sal cupped her shoulders. "Remember what Chantry did. He's not going to change his spots. Not this late in the game."

Resentment welled up inside of her, and she wrenched away. "You think you can just tell me what to do and I'll meekly surrender?"

"You'd never surrender. That's not who you are."

"I don't know who I am." The words were wrenched from her. The past week had stripped away her self-awareness, her confidence, her belief in everything she held dear. "I don't know anything."

"You've had one shock after another. It's no wonder you're questioning things." He took one long stride, closing the distance she had so recently created. "Can't you just accept that I don't want to see you hurt?"

"Of course." Her resolve melted. "I know you only want to protect me. But there are things you can't protect me from."

"Like your need to make things right."

"For one." She bit her lower lip. "I have to decide what's right for me. Bringing Calvin in, putting an end to whatever he was involved in is the right thing to do." She lifted her gaze so that it met his squarely. "If it were you, what would you do?"

She knew the answer before she asked the question. Sal wouldn't hesitate to put his life on the line if it meant protecting others.

'That's different."

"No. It's exactly the same."

"You don't play fair," he said at last.

Olivia knew what she had to do. She'd known it from the moment Sal had told her about the call.

"Set it up with Homeland."

Sal wanted to hit something. Or someone. He watched as a female agent fitted Olivia with a wire.

"I'll be fine," Olivia said. "You'll be able to hear everything that's going on."

"You don't believe Chantry's going to turn himself in." Sal fixed an accusing look on Timmons and Jeppsen.

"No. We don't. What we want from Ms. Hammond is to get a confession on tape. What we know and what we can prove are two different things. We have plenty on him, but a confession will go a long way to proving his guilt. Then we can leverage that to get information on the rest of the cell."

"Don't you think it's about time you told us what Chantry was mixed up in?" Sal demanded. "Olivia's putting her life on the line. She deserves to know."

Jeppsen gave him a long look. "You've heard of HEU?"

Sal nodded. "Highly enriched uranium."

"Got it in one. It takes fifty kilos to create a nuclear detonation. Compare that to the nearly one ton of low-enriched uranium needed to produce just one nuclear bomb and you have an idea of what we're up against. We think Chantry decided to double-cross his partners and hold a bidding war."

Sal gave a low whistle. "No wonder his pals want him so bad."

"This is fissile uranium, meaning it contains more than 85 percent uranium 235. That makes it weapons grade."

Sal had been on enough missions charged with securing uranium storage facilities to understand the difference between weapons grade and weapons usable uranium. The explosion or boom would be smaller with the weapons grade uranium, but the radiation fallout infinitely more devastating, leaving the affected area a wasteland for decades.

Divide it up and spread it over a couple of dozen or so rockets and you could start enough small skirmishes to cause devastation all over the world.

"You can imagine the chaos if our enemies got their hands on it," Jeppsen added. "They plan to start in America."

Sal nodded again, more grimly this time. The effects of an HEU blast would be catastrophic. No wonder Homeland was so intent on stopping the plan.

Olivia forced herself not to fidget with the wire. The slightest movement, the agents had told her, could interfere with the receiving and transmitting.

She walked under the pier, letting her eyesight become accustomed to the near blackness.

"There you are." Calvin's voice.

The air seemed dark and heavy with his presence. How had she not felt it before? He was a chameleon, changing to fit whatever circumstances he found himself in, never showing his true colors because he didn't have any.

"You said you wanted to turn yourself in."

He laughed richly. "You always were a fool, Olivia. You and your father both. You were too busy being the defenders of the underdog, the crusaders for truth and justice and the American way to even notice what was going on right under your noses."

"How long?" she asked, her voice a mere sliver of sound. "How long were you cheating my father?"

"From the beginning."

"No!" She couldn't believe it. Wouldn't.

"Yes. Come closer. I know you're wired."

"What makes you think that?"

"You're the fool. Not me. Homeland's listening in right now." He yanked her arm, pulling her to him, then ripped the collar of her shirt to expose the wire.

When he had it, he pushed her away, his gaze raking her with contempt. "Why did you come? You had to know I wasn't going to turn myself in."

"I wanted to give you the opportunity to do the right thing. You were my father's friend. My friend. That means something."

He snapped his fingers. "That's all your so-called friendship is worth."

"Why did you ask me to come?"

"You signed my death warrant when I didn't get the drive the last time. I'd ask you where you stashed it, but it doesn't matter. My partners didn't take kindly to my trying to cut them out. That's why they came after you. They thought you were part of it." He gave a careless laugh, clearly not at all remorseful that his actions had put her life in jeopardy.

Swallowing her revulsion for the man and his words, she ignored the last. "Homeland will protect you. You can turn state's evidence."

"You think I want to spend the rest of my life in prison?"

"At least you'll be alive."

He pulled a knife. "Did you know that I always hated you and your holier-than-thou father? I hated what you stood for. I hated all the pro bono work you and he insisted we take on. I used to laugh about it. Your father is gone, but I can take my revenge on you."

Instead of backing away as he no doubt expected, she took a step closer and gauged the distance separating them. Her martial arts teacher had more than once commended her on her *mae geri* or front kick.

Five feet. She had to get closer. Keep him talking. Another step. One more should do it. "You must have had yourself a good old time laughing at Daddy and me behind our backs." It didn't require any acting on her part to let the pain show. It was all too real.

"I have to admit to having a chuckle once in a while over all that earnestness you and your old man brought to every case, so eager to see that all those losers had 'legal representation.' Did you ever wonder why I gave you all those bleeding heart cases?"

She paused, wanting to know the answer. "Why did you?"

"So you'd keep your nose out of what I was doing. It was a foolproof way to keep you occupied while I did real business," he bragged and the evil inside him slouched behind his gaze.

And she'd thought he'd believed in her. What a fool she'd been. A trusting, stupid fool. Well, this was one time she wouldn't play the fool. He would. "Real business, meaning dirty business," she translated, inching forward.

"I prefer to think of it as profitable business. The law firm barely makes enough to pay salaries. I wanted more. I needed more." He smiled beatifically. "I deserved more."

He said it all with such matter-of-factness that she could only shake her head inwardly. "So you betrayed your partner, your best friend, all for a few extra dollars?"

"Possessing things—nice things—is in my blood. I came from Southern royalty. Do you really think I could live on the paltry salary I made at that pitiful firm your father and I started? All he could talk about was helping the little people. Well, I was helping all right. I was helping myself."

She wasn't listening. Calvin was a tall man, not as tall as Sal, but tall enough. She'd have to bring her knee up tight and high if she wanted to go for his chin. Which she did.

Her left knee shot up, quickly followed by her leg jerking straight out, the heel of her foot catching him squarely in the jaw.

Contact. The shock of impact shot through her leg and torso. She inhaled sharply but kept her balance.

He howled in rage and surprise and dropped the knife.

She kicked it away and started to turn, preparing to run, but he managed to latch onto her shoulder, fingers digging deep. "Not so fast." His words were slurred, as though it was an effort to speak.

Good. She struggled to free herself, but he was far stronger. "That's going to cost you, Olivia."

Calvin moved his hand to her upper arm and gripped it with careless but cruel strength. "Congratulations on that fancy bit of footwork. Didn't know you had it in you." Reluctant admiration warred with disgust in his voice. Rage, dark and nasty, boiled in his eyes. She would have stepped back from all that hatred if he hadn't tightened his hold so that she couldn't move.

Olivia wanted to weep. She wouldn't get another chance. He'd be on his guard now. Why hadn't she moved sooner? Faster?

Relentlessly, Calvin marched her farther under the pier. When they reached a point she judged to be approximately at the center, he stopped. "This should do."

"Do for what?"

"We don't want any amorous young couples looking for privacy stumbling across us. Not many go this far." He gave a mock shudder. "Too dark."

Olivia did her best to suppress her own shudder. Some kind of creature was making flapping noises. She didn't particularly want to know what it was.

"I didn't give you enough credit. You made a worthy opponent," Calvin said. "More so than I had thought."

"Am I supposed to thank you for the compliment?"

"Flippant to the end. Good for you. You're going to need that when the tide starts to come in."

What did he have in mind? Then she saw it. A coil of rope. He planned to tie her to one of the posts supporting the pier.

She renewed her struggles, but his grip was iron-hard. "Unless you want to bleed to death, you'll keep still." After pulling a knife from his pocket, he nicked sensitive skin beneath her ear to make his point. A warm stickiness trickled down her neck.

"You're a traitor and a murderer." How had she ever thought of him as a friend, a mentor?

"There are all sorts of bad guys in the world. You'll find that I'm one of the lesser ones when you start looking around."

"Is that how you want to be remembered?"

"I want my piece of the pie," he said conversationally as he began binding her to the post. The tide was not in yet, but the lap of it in the distance reminded her that it would soon reach her ankles, her knees.

"The big pie. Not the pennies we make at the firm. Fronting for a few terrorists was an easy way to cut myself a slice or two. All I had to do was grease a few palms and use my contacts to finesse matters. Then I realized I could make even more if I cut the Russians out completely."

Olivia focused on a single word. "Terrorists? As in people who are trying to destroy our country, our way of life? That's who you've cozied up to? What happened to you, Calvin?" She genuinely wanted to know.

"Nothing happened. I'm the same man I always was. You're just now seeing the real me." He laughed, the gleeful sound echoing through the dark.

EIGHTEEN

Sal heard the crackling noise followed by silence and understood what it meant: Chantry had found the wire. Sal didn't wait for the Homeland boys. He'd already taken off, ignoring the shouts of Timmons and Jeppsen.

Silently, he made his way under the pier, crept closer until he heard Chantry's wicked laugh. He squelched the urge to go and yank Olivia from him, but he bided his time. He had been in enough similar situations to know how costly a false move could be. If ever he needed to keep his wits about him, this was it.

Chantry had his back to him, but Olivia had a clear line of sight over the man's shoulder. Look up, Sal silently urged. If she saw him, she'd use it. He knew it. Olivia wasn't one to give up.

He saw the moment she caught sight of him. A tiny nod on her part acknowledged his presence.

"How'd you meet the Russians?" she asked.

Attagirl, Sal silently cheered. Keep him talking.

"Networking. It's all about meeting the right people."

"The right people being those who blow up innocent men, women and children?"

"What do I care about fools who find themselves in the wrong place at the wrong time? Not my problem."

Sal heard the hatred in Chantry's voice, knew that the

man was close to losing control. Once he did, he'd take all that hatred out on Olivia.

Sal was almost there. Another three yards. He could feel Olivia's fear and sent an encouraging smile her way. Everything in him slowed: his heartbeat eased, his blood pressure dropped, his breathing went shallow.

Cold zero.

He was in the zone and was now operating on rote.

Two more steps.

One more.

And he was six feet on the far side of Olivia. Though he was loath to reveal his presence, he knew he had to take Chantry's attention away from her. "That was some stunt, Chantry. You had us all fooled."

Chantry spun, all the while keeping Olivia, who was half-bound to the post, in front of him, the knife poised at the curve of her throat. The rage that bellowed through him reminded Sal of the sound a bull made when he was thwarted in reaching a cow. "You. Why can't you die?"

"Sorry to not oblige."

"It's never too late," Chantry said. "I know what you're doing. Keep your distance or your girlfriend dies." He was sweating profusely, a sign that he was more nervous than he let on.

Okay. Use that against him.

"Who's calling the shots?" Sal asked. "You don't have the moxie to put this together yourself."

"Who're you to tell me what I can or can't do?"

"I just have to look at you to know you're a second-rater." Sal was taking a risk. He knew it. If Chantry got too angry, he'd turn it on Olivia. At the same time, his anger could cause him to make a mistake.

Olivia's blink told Sal she knew what he was doing.

"Put down your weapon," Chantry ordered. "If you value her neck, you'll put it down and kick it over here."

"Don't listen to him," Olivia said. "He plans to kill me whatever you do."

Chantry inched the knife along her throat, drawing a thin line of blood. "She's right."

Sal forced himself not to respond. The sight of Chantry's knife along Olivia's throat terrified him. That's what the man wanted. He wanted Sal to lose his cool, to react to the trail of blood blooming against the paleness of her skin.

"You're boring me," he said.

Chantry's eyes narrowed. "Boring you? We'll have to remedy that. Maybe I'll move the knife a few inches higher. Say, to that beautiful cheekbone."

The sharp intake of Olivia's breath screamed along Sal's nerves. Keep it together, he cautioned himself. He inclined his head, the motion barely perceptible, but Olivia caught it. She blinked in acknowledgment.

"You're a fool, Chantry. Homeland is here."

"You think I don't know? My plan was brilliant and would have worked. If only she—" he pressed the knife to Olivia's neck "—had brought the right USB drive."

"I think you've let your arrogance blind you to everything but what you want to see," Sal said, playing the man. Chantry was an egotist. He had to believe that he was right, that he was invincible. Otherwise, he would see the truth about himself. That he was nothing.

With every word, Sal inched his way closer.

"I made millions. Millions, do you hear me, just for acting as a front man. I could have made even more if I'd held a bidding war with the HEU as the prize." Chantry was incapable of accepting any responsibility and had to lay the blame of his failures on others.

"You were my friend," Olivia said, drawing the man's attention away from Sal's agonizingly slow progress. "You were Daddy's friend."

"He was as big a fool as you. He always was. I was

robbing the firm blind for years, and he was too stupid to see it. He was too busy saving the 'little people.' Like they mattered."

Sal gained a few more inches. Another foot and he'd be in striking distance.

"Daddy knew what was important. He was richer than you could ever be."

Sal made his move. He struck out with his right leg, catching Chantry in the knee. The knee was a particularly sensitive joint, crucial to standing, to balance. Chantry released Olivia and grasped his leg. At that moment, Sal hooked his arm around the man's neck and squeezed.

"You put your hands on Olivia. For that alone, I could kill you."

Chantry was gasping for breath.

"Sal, it's okay. I'm okay," Olivia said, quickly undoing the rope tying her legs to the post. "Let him go. That's not who we are. We're not killers. We're not like him."

Her words penetrated the rage that had fogged his thinking. Sal eased his grip fractionally.

Then it happened. Chantry fell to the ground. Sal recognized the faint pop, a shot from a rifle with a suppressor. He yanked his weapon from his shoulder holster and scanned the surroundings, directing it in a swiveling arc.

No movement betrayed the shooter's position. This was a professional hit. If the killer's end game had been to kill Chantry, he would have already disappeared, but Sal didn't want to risk it. Not with Olivia's life at stake.

He spared a glance at Chantry. The bullet hole made a neat circle in the man's forehead.

"What…" Olivia's voice died as she registered the meaning of the hole.

"I don't know where the shooter is," Sal whispered. At the moment, they were sitting ducks, no cover except for the scant protection of the dead man's body.

He pulled Olivia down with him and pushed her behind Chantry. "Stay down."

Her repugnance at using her onetime friend's body as cover was fully evident in her eyes, but she nodded.

Sal crawled in the direction from which he thought the shot came. High grass effectively blocked his view to the area that flanked the pier.

After spotting nothing, he made his way back to Olivia. "We have to get out of here."

"What about…him?" she asked, gesturing to the lifeless body. And he knew, despite everything Chantry had done, that she mourned his death. It was that grief that would torment her.

"We'll send someone back for him." When I get you somewhere safe, he silently added. He had to get Olivia out of here while shock was still uppermost and she hadn't had time to think. Once she had time to consider what had happened, she'd have difficulty functioning.

They crab-crawled their way from beneath the pier. When they reached the open ground, they stood, stretched cramped muscles.

With one arm wrapped around her, Sal tried his phone and found he had service. He dialed 911 and reported the murder. He figured Timmons and Jeppsen would be along soon enough. Right now, Sal preferred not to have to deal with the DHS agents who had shown such callous disregard for Olivia's life.

"Who…" Olivia's voice trembled. "Who would have done it?"

"At a guess, I'd say the people Chantry was working for. Terrorists don't like failure."

Shock coursed through Olivia as she struggled to wrap her mind around what had happened. First she was held at knifepoint by Chantry, nearly died at his hand, and then

Chantry was shot. The pain of betrayal and loss clawed through her heart, leaving it tattered and bleeding.

In a haze, she half listened while Sal gave the location to the police. He then turned his attention to her. "Are you all right?"

"I don't know," she said honestly. "I thought he was going to kill me and then...and then he was dead."

Sal folded her into his arms. "You're safe now."

She nestled against him, needing his solid strength. "Thank you. You saved my life."

"You saved yourself by keeping Chantry talking. Never underestimate yourself, Olivia. You're one tough lady."

That got a laugh from her. "I'll remember that."

Sal didn't smile. "Make sure that you do."

Timmons and Jeppsen showed up, followed by the police, and Sal excused himself to talk with them, leaving Olivia to ponder what he'd just said.

Deltas were an elite class of men. She had only to look at Sal to know the truth of that. He was carved from integrity and layered in honor. A compliment from him meant something.

She held on to that faith in the next hour.

The staccato give-and-take of the crime scene techs, the flash of strobe lights and the glances darted her way pinged against her senses. She wanted to close her eyes and put her hands over her ears to block everything out.

But that was impossible.

At Sal's insistence, the Homeland agents and police questioned him first. When it was Olivia's turn, she told them about Chantry finding the wire and ripping it from her.

"That's an end to the questions," Sal said. "If you want to ask us anything more, you can wait until morning."

"You'll be hearing from us," Timmons said.

Sal shot a fulminating look his way. "You and your partner almost got Olivia killed. Was it worth it?"

Olivia forced herself to not turn away as Calvin's body was carried from underneath the pier in a black body bag. Calvin was dead. He couldn't hurt her anymore. Even as the thought formed, she knew it wasn't true.

Would the sight of his body being carried away bring her closure? She didn't know. Could she ever think of Calvin without remembering this horrific night, the pinch of his knife at her throat, the rasp of his voice at her ear, laughing, taunting?

He was dead. But it wasn't over.

Hand at her elbow, Sal escorted her to the truck. Once inside, he turned to her. "You look like I could pass my hand right through you."

She managed a husky laugh. "You always did know how to flatter a girl."

"We're going home. There'll be time enough to sort this out once you've had something to eat and some rest."

"And a shower," she said, rubbing her arms. "I feel dirty."

NINETEEN

Shelley called the next morning. "Found it," she said without preamble. "A file on the drive labeled Cerberus." Her voice lowered. "Sal, what are you and Olivia mixed up in? This is serious stuff."

As she took him through it, his lips tightened. Chantry's involvement had extended far beyond simply selling information as the DHS had first said. If Chantry and his partners had succeeded, three major cities in the United States would have been attacked.

"We need to get this to Homeland," Shelley said. "I can send it directly from here."

Sal didn't immediately agree, thinking of Timmons and Jeppsen's treatment of Olivia and the fact that he still didn't know if he could trust them.

"I know people we can trust," Shelley said, sensing his objections.

"Okay. Thanks, boss. You really came through."

"You and Olivia are the ones who came—" A groan he'd come to recognize interrupted whatever she'd been about to say. "Sorry. Another soccer game going on. I don't know who'll be happier when this baby arrives, me or Caleb."

Sal chuckled. "I'm rooting for you."

"I've got an assignment for you when you return. An oil CEO is getting threats and wants S&J to look into them."

"Okay." Sal hadn't thought of when he'd return to Atlanta, but he knew now that he needed to consider it. The truth was, he didn't want to leave Olivia.

When he'd taken her home last night, she'd been white with exhaustion and grief. She needed something to take her mind off the knowledge that a man she'd considered a friend had betrayed her and then tried to kill her.

Sal didn't do comfort. It wasn't part of the Delta skill set. In his family, food was comfort. His mother, a true Southern cook, had served up biscuits and gravy or spaghetti and red sauce along with love and practical advice whenever a crisis hit. With Sal and his brother and three sisters, crises were a way of life in the Santonni household.

He wasn't a cook, no more than passable, but he could order from a deli just fine. So that was what he did.

He found a deli, ordered the sides for an old-fashioned picnic and then paid extra to the helpful lady behind the counter to arrange everything so it looked pretty in the basket he'd brought with him. To his way of thinking, a picnic wasn't a picnic without a basket and a red plaid blanket.

He showed up at Olivia's place with the packed basket and a jug of lemonade and a goal to take her away from her grief if only for a few hours. He couldn't give her a future together, but he could give her today.

"Grab your jacket," he said. "We're going on a picnic." He tried not to wince at the dark circles that underscored her eyes.

"A picnic?"

"Sure. Fried chicken, potato salad, dill pickles and chocolate chip cookies. The works."

"When did you manage to do this?"

Sal shook his head. "I didn't make it. But I did have the idea. Do I get points?" he asked, hoping to raise a smile from her.

"You've gone to a lot of trouble," Olivia said. "And I

thank you for it. Really, I do." Her voice cracked a bit. "But I'm afraid I'm not in a picnic mood." Her shoulders, usually held so proudly straight, drooped.

"That's when you need a picnic most of all."

The smile he'd hoped for peeked out in bits and pieces. "You're right. I do need a picnic. I just didn't know it." With that, she put her hands on his shoulders and tilted her head up so that her eyes met his. "Thank you. Seriously, thank you."

He brushed his lips over hers. She didn't resist but, instead, melted into the kiss, into him. He held her gently. She'd lost weight she couldn't afford to lose and felt fragile in his arms.

She must have guessed at his thoughts for she smiled up at him. "I'm not delicate, Sal. It might seem so right now, but I'm still standing. I won't let this defeat me. Calvin was never my friend. Not really. So I didn't lose him, because how can I lose something that never existed in the first place?"

"Your logic is irrefutable."

Her smile grew.

She was right, he thought. She *was* still standing. And he was proud of her in a way that felt very personal, very possessive.

How would she feel if he told her just that? But now wasn't the time to tell her of those feelings. Now was the time for a picnic under the sun, with chicken eaten with fingers, creamy potato salad and cookies chunky with chocolate pieces.

First, though, he needed to tell Olivia what Shelley had discovered. Better to get it out of the way now and not spoil their picnic.

"Shelley called. She found an encrypted file on the drive labeled Cerberus." Sal swallowed, not wanting to tell Olivia the rest.

"There's more, isn't there?"

"Chantry and his pals were planning to target three American cities. If they'd succeeded, Chantry stood to earn five million dollars for his part, courtesy of the Russians. If he'd managed to hold the bidding war he'd planned, he'd make two, three times that." Sal let the starkness of the words stand. There was no way to pretty them up.

She shook her head as though to negate the evidence, and Sal understood that she was trying to come to grips with further proof that the man she'd looked up to could have been involved in such a heinous plot. No wonder the plot was code-named Cerberus. Like the three-headed mythological creature, there were three cities targeted.

"Thank you for telling me. I know it wasn't easy for you, but I needed to know." Olivia held her head high and gave a bright smile. "I won't let him ruin our day. He's taken too much already."

Sal's admiration for her rose another notch. She'd taken the news hard, but she hadn't let it defeat her.

"You're good to me," Olivia said as he helped her into the truck. "Good for me," she added when he climbed in the driver's side and buckled up.

Sal didn't let himself think beyond the next few hours.

They drove to a spot tucked on the crest of a gentle hill where they could look out at the city.

Determined to enjoy the day, Olivia shook away the grief over Calvin that had clung to her like a burr. What sleep she'd managed to get last night had been punctuated with accusations, from the agents, from herself.

Enough.

She and Sal deserved a few hours of happiness, free from terrorist plots and a friend's betrayal.

The day was dusted with magic. Olivia and Sal attacked the chicken with the enthusiasm of hungry children, un-

ashamedly licking their fingers. They consumed the potato salad and pickles and argued good-naturedly over
who got the last cookie.

Replete with good food, Olivia stretched out on the
blanket and stared at the late afternoon sky.

The clouds were those perfect, dreamy ones, resem-
bling giant marshmallows floating in a sky so blue that
it hurt the eyes.

She wanted to bottle the day and preserve it as she'd
seen her mother bottle peaches and pears. Rows of canned
fruit had marched across the old-fashioned sideboard in
the kitchen. A pang of loss seized Olivia as she thought of
her mother, too soon gone at only forty years old.

She shook off the momentary sadness and concentrated
on the man who sat cross-legged across from her. With
a start, she accepted that she'd fallen in love with Sal all
over again. Only this time, her feelings went far deeper.
She knew the suffering he'd endured over his service to
his country, the pain he still carried with him. It only made
her love him more. She wanted to shout her love to the sky.

The remote expression in his eyes, though, kept the
words locked inside of her. "Thank you for a perfect day."

"My pleasure."

The words were right, but something was wrong with
the tone. She tried to discover what was off, but there was
nothing she could pinpoint.

"Two years ago, when we were together, you made my
heart do funny things."

"Funny how?"

"You made it flutter." She waved her fingers. "But now
it's more. It's more real. And stronger. And I don't know
what to do with it. Except this." She sat up and touched
her lips to his. Everything she felt for him, for the man he
was, filled her.

She caught his hand, laced her fingers with his. Palm

to palm, she thought. It didn't matter that his much bigger hand swallowed her own. Nor did it matter that his darker skin contrasted with the paleness of hers. All that mattered was that they were there, linked in all the important ways.

Gently, Sal pulled away.

The sun sank deep into the horizon, spilling fire and gold onto the landscape. Olivia spared a moment to absorb it, though even the compelling beauty of the sunset couldn't penetrate the darkness that had moved into the day and her heart.

She felt Sal withdrawing from her. With every look, he moved another step from her. And she didn't know why.

Was it worry over the terrorists' plot that had caused him to withdraw? After he'd told her what Shelley had found on the drive, they hadn't talked about Calvin or the Russians, neither wanting such ugliness to intrude upon the day.

Once she'd started to bring it up, then thought better of it. There'd be time enough to deal with the implications of Calvin's involvement when she and Sal returned home. She'd tried to call Walter, to express her sympathy, but, once again, received no answer.

She didn't blame him for not wanting to take any calls. Calvin's part in the terrorist plot had become common knowledge. That, compounded by his death, must be eating away at his son.

She glanced at Sal, saw the bleakness in his eyes. Was it something more personal that had caused him to withdraw? Whatever it was, she felt a frisson of foreboding skate down her spine. Just when she thought they'd reached some kind of understanding, he closed himself off. It didn't make sense.

His hands on her shoulders, he lowered his head and brushed his lips over hers.

Her heart tripped in her throat, part nerves, part pleasure, part satisfaction. The kiss was everything she'd remembered. And more. More than the kisses of two years ago.

She wondered at that. Was the more—and it was definitely more—because they had both grown in the intervening years? Or was it because they had faced danger together and come out on the other end?

Did he know that her heart bounced around in her chest like a child's ball, or that nerves raced over her skin, making her hot and cold at the same time? Did he know that he had only to look at her and she shivered with pleasure?

She wasn't sure. She only knew that in his arms, she was at home. She tried to convince herself that she was wrong about his distancing himself from her. Surely he could not have kissed her as he had if he didn't care for her, love her.

When Sal touched his lips to hers, he tasted his own desperation, his fading hope that he and Olivia could have a life together. Lastly, he tasted bitterness. His own. He was damaged in ways he feared could never be healed.

He lifted his head and saw the wonder and love in Olivia's gaze. He should never have kissed her, but he'd been unable to resist. "We should go."

There was a quiet intimacy in the cab of the truck. He let it wrap its way around him. When they reached the city, he would tell her. She would protest, might even cry a little, but in the end, she would acknowledge that it was for the best, maybe even be a little relieved.

Yes, he'd made the right choice.

Life would return to normal. Olivia would go back to her job and fight for those who couldn't fight for themselves, and he would return to Atlanta, to his life there. In many ways, it was a good life. He had work he enjoyed, friends who were there for him when he needed them, which wasn't often, but still, it was good to know they were there.

And he wondered who he was trying to convince that he wanted that life. He'd been content, if not happy, up until Olivia's call. It had changed everything.

As they made the return trip to Olivia's townhome, Sal felt her questioning gaze on him. He knew he was sending mixed signals. How did he tell her that he had nothing to give her?

Olivia was everything he'd ever wanted in a woman, ever dreamed of, and he couldn't have her. Because he loved her, he would walk away. Never mind that it would tear the heart from him.

He would do it because he didn't have another choice. His soul was filled with a darkness so intense that sometimes he feared it would consume him.

Olivia deserved better.

TWENTY

Once home, Olivia emptied the picnic basket. "Thank you for today. I didn't know how much I needed it."

Sal stood by the window, his back to her. "We both did."

She sniffed the leftover potato salad, decided it smelled iffy and put it in the trash. "What's next for you?"

"I head back to Atlanta."

"So soon?" She hoped her voice didn't give away her dismay.

"It's time. I have to get back to work."

"Of course." He'd stayed in Savannah for a week, far longer than either of them had foreseen when she'd called him.

"I'm glad we found the truth. That's what matters." He swung back to her. His face looked ravaged.

"And us?" She dared to utter the question that had swelled inside of her for the last two days. Ever since the scene at the pier, Sal had pulled steadily away from her until she felt as though they were strangers. "What about us?"

She thought she had her answer, but, perversely, she wanted him to say the words. "You and me. Are we over, too?"

"Livvie." If she'd doubted where she stood with him, the single word said it all. There was resignation there. Maybe even a touch of sadness. "We were over two years ago."

"I thought… I thought things had changed."

"Nothing's changed. We're still the same people. You'll go back to fighting for the underdog and I…"

"And you'll what?" She closed the few steps between them and laid her hand on his arm. "What will you do?"

"Shelley told me she had a new case for me. The CEO of an oil company received some threats and wants someone to look into it."

"Is that what you want?"

"Whatever this thing is, it can't go anywhere. You know what I did when I was overseas. I didn't just kill the enemy. I spotted them for the snipers."

"You did your job, the job your superiors assigned you. What would you say to a soldier who had done the same thing? Would you condemn him?"

"Of course not. He was following orders."

"Then what makes it any different for you?" She let that sink in. "You think you're better than the next guy? Then why are you holding yourself to a different set of standards?"

"You're twisting everything up."

"Am I?" She paused. "Or are you? You saved lives by doing what you did. You have to know that. In my book, that makes you a hero. Why can't you show the same compassion to yourself that you showed to the children in Afghanistan? To your buddies?"

Sal didn't respond, and she didn't press. He needed to see in himself what she saw.

"I'm not a hero, so don't make me out to be one." He paced. "I'm not the right man for you. Your faith is a part of you. Mine died a long time ago. Don't you get it? I'm broken inside. Nothing will put me back together." The laugh he gave held not a whit of humor. Bitterness rang from its hollow tone. "I can't ask you to stick around and watch as I fall apart."

"What if I want to?"

"Then you're a fool."

The harshness of the words had her shrinking back. Calvin had said the same thing to her. Had it only been last night? "Why can't you see yourself as I do? A strong man who did his best under intolerable conditions."

"Don't make this any harder than it has to be. You'll go back to your life. And I'll go back to mine."

"I love you. Nothing's going to change that. Not even you." It was her turn to move to the window and turn her back to him. "I love you. I always have."

"This isn't the time…"

"It's exactly the time." She spun around, stood on tiptoe to touch her lips to his. "I love you."

"You don't know what you're saying. You're feeling grateful. That isn't love."

"I'm not a child. I know the difference between gratitude and love."

"Do you? We haven't had a normal moment since this all began. You can't trust what you're feeling."

"Maybe it's you I can't trust."

He sucked in a hard breath at that. "Olivia…"

"Don't. Just don't."

"We can talk it out. You'll see that I'm right."

"Unless you can believe that I love you, we have nothing to talk about. You were a Delta, but you're running scared. Of me. Of what we could have together."

"There is no 'together.' Not for us."

"Is that what you want?"

"It's what has to be."

"I love you. If you're too much of a coward to accept it, then you're not the man I thought you were."

"I can't stay. I'd make you miserable."

"Don't you dare speak for me. We could have something good. Build a life together. But you won't let yourself see what we have. It's one thing to push me away. I hope you don't do the same with the Lord. Because however much I love you, He loves you infinitely more."

She sensed the internal struggle going on within Sal. Just when she thought he might accept what she was saying, he took a step back, putting an unbreachable distance between them. In that instant, any hope she had died.

"I can't leave you alone tonight. Whoever killed Chantry is still out there."

"He has no reason to come after me. Not anymore. Go home, Sal. There's no place for you here."

From the window, Olivia watched him walk away. When he disappeared from sight, she pressed her head against the pane of glass. She massaged her temples, back and forth, back and forth, as though the repetitive action could erase the pain.

She fisted her hands at her sides and thought about why Sal had turned away from her. He'd given the standard "It's not you, it's me" speech, but was it true? Maybe she was wrong about his feelings and he really didn't love her. Had she ever considered the possibility? As she thought about it, she realized he'd never said those three all-important words.

At the time, she'd thought it was his reluctance to give voice to his feelings, but now she knew differently. The pain of Sal's leaving her two years ago was nothing compared to this new heartache.

For as long as she could remember, she had struggled for perfection, in her personal and her professional life. Failure was anathema to her, and she had definitely failed in her relationships.

She hadn't set out to fall in love with Salvatore Santonni, but love had stolen into her heart, even when it wasn't returned.

Love wasn't convenient. It was messy, complicated and,

at times, painful. There were still things they would have needed to talk through. The big and little things that couples who cared about each other shared and discussed, worked through and managed.

She and Sal could have handled those, if only he'd give them a chance. That was what hurt the most: he had refused to give them a chance.

Her childhood dreams of finding her Prince Charming, perfect in every way, had been replaced by something far more substantial and infinitely more dear. She'd found that she didn't need a perfect man; she only needed the one who was perfect for her.

He didn't believe it. He saw only darkness in himself. He didn't see what she did. He didn't see the courageous man who had given everything for his country, including parts of his soul. He didn't see the compassion that shone from his eyes or the simple goodness that colored everything he did. He was a true hero in every sense of the word.

She knew one thing for certain. Nothing would ever be the same.

Sal forced himself to walk away. From Olivia. From the life they might have had if his soul had not been so scarred. As long as he focused on what was best for her, he was able to put one foot in front of the other. He had to steer away from the minefield of what he wanted for himself.

He longed to believe her, to believe they had a future together. Intending to call her, he picked up the phone, aching to hear her voice. And set it down again. Nothing had changed from when he'd left her two years ago. He was still the same man he had been, flawed and imperfect.

There'd been stark pain in Olivia's voice when she'd ordered him to leave. He'd done that. He had to live with the knowledge. But how much worse for her would it be if she were to marry him and had to endure the darkness that lived inside of him?

He couldn't do that to her. Wouldn't.

What he felt for her terrified him because for every ounce of love he had for her, he felt…knew…simultaneously that he wasn't worthy.

Leaving Olivia was the right thing to do, even if it wrenched the heart from him. Though they couldn't be together, he still needed to make certain she was safe.

He called Nicco, who freelanced for S&J when they needed an operative in Savannah.

"I need a favor."

Grateful that it was Sunday and she didn't have to show up for work, Olivia showered and then dressed in a pair of jeans and a pink top. She needed to take in all that had happened over the last week: Calvin's betrayal and death, and, more important, Sal's rejection.

She tackled Calvin first. For her own peace of mind, she had to believe that he'd once been a good man, the man she remembered. He'd allowed the lure of easy money, the quick score, the big and shiny to take him down the wrong path. He wouldn't be the first to succumb to such temptation.

As for Sal, she just wanted to weep. He'd turned away from her and what they might have had. She hadn't been enough for him to put away the past.

The ringing of the doorbell had her checking the peephole, then opening the door as she recognized Nicco Santonni.

She hadn't paid a lot of attention to Sal's younger brother earlier and now gave him closer scrutiny. Though not as tall as Sal, Nicco still topped six feet easily. The dark hair and darker eyes said "Santonni," as did the off-center dimple in his chin.

He had a fresh-faced look about him, she thought, until she looked more deeply and saw the telltale lines fanning from the corners of his eyes, eyes that said he had seen more than his share of suffering. Sal had told her once that Nicco had served with the Rangers, the cause of a good-natured rivalry between the brothers.

"Sal sent me. Said maybe you and I might hang out for a while."

"You mean he asked you to keep an eye on me."

The dimple winked as he grinned. "He might have said something about that."

She bit back the cry that threatened to spill from her lips. Sal didn't want her, but he'd sent his brother to watch over her? The irony of it was too much.

"Please, Olivia. Big brother will have my hide if I don't do what he says."

When he put it that way, she couldn't refuse. "Come in." She flushed at the grudging tone. "Thank you for coming. You didn't have to."

For the next hour, Nicco did his best to entertain her. While she appreciated his efforts, she didn't need or want to be entertained.

Olivia tried to shake off the depression that had swallowed her whole. Sal didn't want a future with her. He'd made that plain. She wasn't doing herself or anybody else any good moping, so she tried to engage herself in the board game Nicco had found in her hall closet.

He moved a piece. "I win," he crowed.

Despite her heartache, she laughed. "How do you know you won? Neither one of us can figure out the rules."

It felt good. The laughter. "Thank you. I needed that."

"My pleasure." Nicco pushed aside the game and looked at her with eyes so much like his brother's that she wanted to cry. "Whatever Sal did, he did because he loves you."

"You're wrong there. He doesn't want anything to do with me."

Whatever Nicco had been about to say was interrupted by the ringing of his phone.

She watched as consternation settled on his features as he spoke. "What is it?" she asked once he'd hung up.

"It's my father. Mama took him to the hospital. Chest pains. She says it's not serious, but she's scared. I hear it in her voice. She can't get a hold of Sal or my sisters."

"Go. I'll be fine here."

He looked torn. "I promised Sal I'd stay with you."

"I'll be fine," she repeated. "You need to be with your parents."

"Stay inside. Lock the doors. Don't let anyone in. I'll be back as soon as I can."

Olivia locked the door behind him and wondered what she'd do with the rest of the day. When her phone rang, she picked it up eagerly, hoping, praying it was Sal.

A glance at the caller ID showed that it was Walter.

When you're feeling blue, do something for somebody else. Her father's words bolstered her, so when Walter asked if she'd visit him, she said yes. How must the son be feeling upon learning what his father had done? Add to that Calvin's murder, and Walter must be devastated.

She scribbled a message for Nicco and tacked it to the door. *Went to see Chantry's son. Be back soon.* She set out for Walter's place but knew a momentary qualm. Calvin was dead. Whoever killed him was still out there, but he'd have no interest in her, she assured herself. Not anymore.

There was no harm in going to see a friend.

TWENTY-ONE

Sal left the hospital after visiting his father. It hadn't been a heart attack after all, but severe indigestion. His father was blustering that he was fine and wanted to go home. With the encouragement of his wife, children and the doctors, he'd been convinced to stay overnight.

"Think of Mama," Sal had said in a coaxing voice to his stubborn father. "She'll worry herself sick if you come home too soon."

"Listen to Sal," Mama said. "He makes good sense."

Upon finding Nicco there, Sal knew he had to get to Olivia.

He was the last person she'd want to see, but he couldn't let her be alone. The gunman who'd killed Chantry was probably long gone, but Sal wasn't taking any chances. Not with Olivia.

As he sped to her townhome, his thoughts spun in a whirlpool of uncertainty. It wasn't regret that sucked him in; it was shame. He hadn't felt that for a long time, but he recognized it immediately. He'd turned away the love of a good woman, the woman he loved, because he was a coward.

He'd have flattened any man who dared to call him that, but he couldn't deny the charge now. He'd been afraid to accept what Olivia offered, afraid that he couldn't live up to the image she had of him. So what had he done? Thrown her love back in her face.

Much of the guilt, the rage, the grief he'd felt over his actions during his time in Afghanistan had dissolved. Olivia had given him that. Then she'd issued a challenge. Coward that he was, he'd rejected it.

When his normally robust father lay in the hospital bed, pale and wan, Sal had come to grips with the fragility of life. He could continue in his self-imposed isolation or he could reach for life and light. With Olivia.

Now he was ready to accept it, to accept the love she offered, if she'd give him another chance. It was time he got on with the business of living and that meant learning to let go.

When he was with Olivia, he felt whole.

A quick read of the note on her front door had him scowling. Why hadn't she stayed at home? He needed to head to Walter's house to find her. When he knew she was safe, he could tell her how he felt.

Walter welcomed her warmly. "Thank you for coming. Learning about Dad and all… I needed someone. You were the first person I thought of."

At any other time, Olivia would have been flattered, but her heartache was too new, too raw to fully register the words. "You're welcome." Walter was a friend and he needed her. "Anything I can do, you know I'll do it."

"I always loved that about you." Walter looked away. "When the news broke about Dad, a lot of people suddenly decided they're too busy to see me."

She didn't know what to say to that. "Give them time," she said at last.

Walter's raised brow confirmed just how weak that sounded.

"I'm sorry. I don't know what you're feeling. I can only

guess. But please know that I'm here for you. Whatever you need, whenever you need it."

Walter grasped her hands. "You always were a good friend. The last years… I let so many things go. I could see Dad slipping further into a web of his own making. I tried… I tried to stop him, but nothing I said made a difference." His voice caught on the last word.

Olivia's heart ached for him.

Walter swiped a hand across his brow. "The press has been brutal. I suppose he deserves it. Still, seeing his name splashed across the papers as some kind of monster… I've been thinking of getting away. Taking a trip. Somewhere. Anywhere."

"That's good. You need time to heal. Away from here and all the memories."

Walter's laugh was hardly more than a cough. "There's no getting away from memories. We carry them around with us, whether or not we want to."

"You're right. I'm sorry. I'm making a mess of things."

The ugly word that spilled from Walter's mouth startled her. He'd always been such a gentleman. Of course, so had Calvin.

He grimaced. "Now it's my turn to apologize. The stress is getting to me."

"Of course." She looked about, saw the sink full of dishes, the cluttered counters. "Why don't I straighten up in here?"

"That's not why I asked you to come. Can we just talk?"

For the next thirty minutes, they talked of inconsequential things until Olivia realized she was doing most of the talking. She picked up her keys. "I should be going."

"So soon?"

"If you want me to stay…"

"Please. As I said, I haven't seen or talked to anyone."

He shook his head. "All of this over some files." Another shake. "Dad must have lost his mind."

Encouraged, Olivia leaned forward. "That's the best way to think of what he did. Remember the man who was your father and took you fishing and taught you how to ride a bike. Let the rest go." She knew, better than most, how difficult that was, but she wanted it for Walter. No child should have to remember his parent as a traitor, a murderer.

A phone rang. Walter looked momentarily annoyed. "Sorry. I'd better get that. Business." He disappeared into another room.

Olivia walked around the great room, approving the rows of bookshelves and the untreated windows that let the morning light spill through. A Cerberus figure in bronze caught her attention.

She picked it up. It was identical to the one Calvin had prized so much. It didn't mean anything, she told herself. Cerberus was a common figure in mythology. There was no reason to believe that Walter was involved with terrorists simply because he had a cheaply made trinket exactly like his father's and that it bore the same name as the file on the jump drive.

A coincidence. That was all.

There are no coincidences. Sal's words came back to taunt her. No. Not Walter. It couldn't be.

She searched for another explanation, any explanation but the one that was staring her in the face. For the second time in less than a week, her heart twisted with the acceptance that someone she'd thought of as a friend had deceived and betrayed her.

Walter turned, saw what she was staring at. "You saw it. Too bad." And the shadow of greed and deceit moved into his eyes. Gone was the boy who had once taught her to skip rocks across a stream. In his place was a man she didn't know, didn't want to know.

She pretended ignorance. "What is it?"

The last vestiges of warmth vanished from his eyes. "You know what it is. It's what this is all about. Dad left the bronze with me for safekeeping. Looks like it's mine for keeps now."

"But you…you aren't a part of it."

The harsh laugh gave her his answer. "I asked you to come here to see what you knew. I should have left good enough alone." He shook his head, negating his words. "No. That's a lie. I wanted you to know. I wanted you to see what I've done, that by tomorrow I'll have pulled off one of the biggest terrorist plots to take place on American soil."

She tried to process it. "You're bragging about it? Bragging about being part of something that will kill hundreds—thousands—of innocent people?"

"Why not?"

"And Calvin? You and he were working together all this time?" She'd thought they weren't that close. It turned out father and son were closer than she'd ever imagined.

"Yeah. We discovered we had a common interest after all. Making money. Did you think dear old Dad knew how to make millions? I showed him how we could by acting as the go-between for the Russians. He wasn't about to give that up. Only trouble was the old man got greedy. He wanted more."

Olivia tried to make sense of his words. "You turned against your own country? You were a SEAL."

He lifted a shoulder in a negligent shrug. "It was either join the service or go to jail. I chose the former."

"Go to jail?" Her head was spinning with every word he uttered.

"Remember that little scrape I was in fifteen years back?"

She probed her memory. "Some misunderstanding about a car, wasn't it?"

"Yeah. Only it wasn't a misunderstanding. I stole the

car. Turns out that it belonged to a city councilman. He was out for blood, but good old Dad intervened, said how I was only acting out after losing my mother." Another laugh. "Wasn't true, of course. I couldn't stand the old bat. But I faked a few tears, said I didn't know what I was doing. It kept me out of jail, provided I enlist."

Olivia recalled that Calvin's wife had died fifteen years ago from an allergic reaction to penicillin. A quick calculation put Walter at nineteen at the time.

"So, no. I didn't enlist because of Mom, flag and apple pie. It worked out pretty good. Turns out I had a knack for manipulating numbers on invoices. I learned how to scam everyone, from the mess hall cook to the sergeant over our platoon. When I got shipped overseas, I started selling on the black market. It came out, of course, but no one wanted it to get out that one of the almighty SEALs was nothing but a common hustler."

She recoiled from his words, from the ugly look in his eyes. How had she ever thought she'd known him? He was a stranger.

"The lady's shocked. I guess I should apologize."

"The lady's repulsed," she said baldly and backed away from him.

"Where do you think you're going?" He took two long strides, grabbed her arms. "You and I are taking a little trip together."

She tried to pull away from him, but he was too strong. "I'm not going anywhere with you."

"Think again." He pulled a syringe from his pocket. "I thought this might come in handy. Turns out I was right." Before she could react, he pressed it against her arm.

Olivia felt herself falling into a sea of blackness.

Sal needed help.

He'd driven to Walter's place, found the house empty and

Olivia's car parked out front. Olivia wasn't answering her cell; his calls had gone directly to voice mail. His anxiety grew with every moment.

If she didn't want to talk with him, fine. But if it was something more… He couldn't shake the feeling of foreboding.

He set aside his animosity for the DHS agents and punched in the number he had for Timmons. A terse explanation later, he did recon outside Walter's house while he waited for the agents to show up, and found a set of tracks heading west. He recalled that a Land Rover had been parked outside Walter's house when he and Olivia had visited there.

The son had to be torn up about what his father had done. Who could blame him? Calvin Chantry had not only broken the law, he'd sold out his country. For an ex-SEAL like Walter, that must have cut deeply.

Sal clenched and unclenched his fingers. He had no need to keep his eye on the clock. His internal timing knew exactly how many minutes, how many hours had passed since Olivia had gone missing. It was a skill born of long hours of watch duty. When a soldier was waiting for something big to happen, he allowed his mind to lock into the steady rhythm of passing minutes and seconds.

Ten minutes later, Timmons and Jeppsen arrived.

Sal took them through the steps that had brought him here. "There's no sign of Walter or Olivia," Sal said, voice tight with worry.

Sal saw the look the agents exchanged. Their grim faces matched the fear that had settled in his chest. "What aren't you telling me?"

The agents looked at each other, looked at him. "We suspect Walter Chantry is part of the terrorist cell," Timmons said at last.

Sal exploded. "You didn't see fit to tell us?"

"It's need-to—"

"Need-to-know. I get it. Your precious need-to-know might cost Olivia her life."

"Look," Timmons said wearily. "We're sorry. But we had orders."

Sal ignored that. He had no idea where Olivia was, and what was more, he didn't know if she was even alive. His entire world had narrowed to finding her. If he lost her… He didn't finish the thought. He didn't think he could bear where it would take him. And he did something he hadn't done in a very long time: he prayed.

Lord, I could really use some help right about now. Olivia's missing and I don't have a clue where she is. Please take care of her until I can find her.

Her life depended upon his ability to disregard the emotions threatening to consume him and to rely upon the training that had been drilled into him. He was no good to Olivia if he went off half-cocked. He took a breath. Another. Never had a mission been more important.

Think. Find a way. Assessing and evaluating before the beginning of an op were among his top strengths as a Delta.

"Chantry's got her. I know it. He's got nothing to lose by killing her."

Timmons held up a hand. "Assuming you're right, how do you suppose we find her?"

Sal forced himself to think like the soldier he was and did what he was trained to do: stay calm, stay ready, stay alert. His muscles relaxed, his breathing became slow and even. Burning his energy with useless worry wouldn't help Olivia.

He told Timmons and Jeppsen of the tracks he'd spotted. "His Land Rover leaves distinctive tracks. We follow them."

"I'll call for reinforcements," Timmons said and punched in a series of numbers. "It'll take them a while."

"I'm not waiting. They can follow when they get here." Sal divided a hard look between the two agents. "Are you coming?"

Part of him wanted to go off on his own, but he reminded himself that he'd been successful in Delta because he was a member of a team. The unit had operated as one, with each man performing his duty.

"We're with you," Timmons said.

It was slow going, but they managed to follow the tracks to the edge of the marsh where they found the Land Rover.

The three men climbed out of the truck. Sal scanned the vast area. Crushing guilt filled him. The combined weight of his Delta uniform, M4 tactical vest, M9 holstered at his hip, and an eighty-pound backpack had nothing on the one sitting on his chest right now. If he'd stayed with Olivia, protected her as he'd promised to do, she wouldn't now be at the mercy of a man like Walter Chantry.

"There's tens of thousands of acres of marsh. How're we supposed to find one woman?" Jeppsen demanded.

"We do whatever it takes."

The agent had the grace to dip his head. "Yeah. Okay."

A shot pierced the air. Clutching his shoulder, Jeppsen fell. A grimace of pain crossed his face as he tried to stand, fell back.

After making certain Timmons had taken cover and pulling Jeppsen behind a log, Sal returned fire. He recognized the futility of it, though, as he couldn't make out the shooter in the dense forest and thick mist.

When the shooting stopped, Sal knelt at Jeppsen's side to check the wound, saw that it was through-and-through. It would hurt, but it wasn't life-threatening.

"Sorry. I'm afraid I'm out of commission for the time being," the agent said between gritted teeth.

After Sal tore a sleeve from his shirt and pressed it against the wound, he and Timmons searched for the shooter.

"He's too good," Sal said in disgust as he combed the forest in vain for any tracks. "Not even a bent blade of grass."

"Probably the same man who took out Chantry at the pier."

Sal and Timmons made a camouflage of leaves and branches to protect Jeppsen.

"Go," Jeppsen urged. "I'll be all right."

It went against Sal's code of honor to leave a man behind, but he nodded. They had to find Olivia. Sooner rather than later. He had no idea whether they were battling two enemies or if the Russians and Walter were working together. Either way, it left Olivia squarely in the middle.

TWENTY-TWO

Her thinking still syrupy from whatever drug Walter had injected her with, Olivia trudged through the marsh, Walter prodding her when her footsteps lagged.

The marsh, a beautiful and wild place, had always filled her with a combination of awe and fear. Swamp gases invaded her nostrils, making her want to gag. Animal sounds caused her to shiver at the thought of what creatures lurked in the deep greenery.

Wisteria grew freely along with honeysuckle, the soft scent a contrast to the hard man who marched her over the rough ground.

"Why?" The question ripped from her throat. "Why, Walter? You were Savannah's golden boy." Walter had graduated at the top of his class and had gone on to serve in the SEALs, had returned with honors and now ran one of the most successful investment banking companies in the South.

"The same reason as my old man, money. Lots and lots of money. More money than you can dream of."

"You have money."

Walter's laugh was totally devoid of humor but held a kind of crude pleasure, making it clear that he was enjoying her fear and revulsion. "There's money. And then there's money. Real money."

"We were friends. We grew up together." She tried to make her words count for more, as though they were a long speech rather than just two short sentences. Tried to make them into an impassioned argument that would sway him from his purpose.

"Funny. Is that how you remember it? 'Cause I don't. I was never good enough for you. Your daddy made that pretty clear."

"We were like brother and sister." The thought of there being something else between them had never entered her mind.

"None of that matters now," he said. "You know too much."

"I don't know anything." But she could guess.

"Give it a rest," Walter said. "You never could lie."

He was right about that.

"What are you going to do?"

"What dear old Dad should have done in the first place. Make sure that you're out of the picture." He paused for effect. "Permanently."

The implication hung as thick and heavy as the humid air that was rank with rotting vegetation.

She had to try one more time to reach him. This was the boy who had helped her catch her first fish. He'd even baited the hook for her when she was too squeamish to do it herself.

As if guessing what was going through her mind, Walter shook his head. "Don't even try."

"Try what?" She made her voice as innocent as she could.

"Making me remember the good old days. From where I'm sitting, they weren't all that good."

Had it all been an act? Calvin and her father. Walter and her. Why hadn't she seen the darkness behind the easy smiles of father and son? Was she so anxious for more family that she'd let herself be blinded to the truth?

"And your father? What about him? Was he ever a friend to my dad? To me?" She willed Walter to say that it hadn't all been an act, that Calvin truly had been sick at the end.

"What do you think?" Walter's careless answer was but one more dart to her heart.

"Calvin wasn't always that way," Olivia argued. "He was my father's best friend. My friend."

Walter laughed. "He used to laugh about putting something over on your father in the business, said he was so trusting that fooling him was child's play. Dad was skimming from the books from the beginning."

No wonder her father had never had two dimes to rub together. Had he suspected that his partner, his best friend was cheating him? A shiver worked its way down Olivia's spine. It looked like father and daughter had been duped by Calvin and Walter.

"My old man was as wily as they came. He played your father. And then you. He taught me along the way. Like how to stay one step ahead of anyone who might come looking for me."

"Who's looking for you?"

He threw her an impatient look. "The Russians. Because dear old Dad tried to double-cross them, they figure they'll take their pound of flesh out of me.

"You're just like your old man," Walter continued. "Both of you look at the world through rose-colored glasses. And now it's going to cost you. Big-time."

"What do you mean?"

"I mean," Walter said, "that you're not going to be found for a long, long time." He gestured with the knife to the marsh. "If ever. The marsh doesn't like to give up its secrets. Too many critters there just waiting for a tasty morsel to snack on."

The shiver of a moment ago morphed into a full-blown shudder. She couldn't help it. The marsh had always terrified her. Ever since she was a child and had gotten lost in the soupy fog, she had been afraid of it.

Buck up, girl. She was no longer a child. She was a grown woman.

"Are you going to knife me in the back?" she challenged. "Where's the sport in that?"

Walter pulled a crossbow from his pack. "I had something a little more sporting in mind. We're going to have us a little hunt. Here's how it'll go: I'll be the hunter and you'll be the hunted." He laughed at the last, then slapped her on the back, pushing her forward. "You've got a five-minute head start."

"You can't be serious."

"Want to stay around and find out?" He checked his watch. "Four minutes and forty seconds. Time's a-wasting."

She stumbled over an exposed root. In trying to catch herself, she grabbed hold of a broken branch. She turned and swung it as she would a club. It wasn't thick enough to pack a lot of wallop, but it made a rewarding whack as it connected with Walter's temple. It didn't topple him, but it stunned him. A small victory for her.

Walter stood, put a hand to his head. It came away bloody. "You always did have your share of guts. Good. You're gonna need them."

Olivia started running. She had no doubt that Walter would do just as he said.

She ran as fast as she could, scrambling over roots and rotted trees. Branches whipped against her face, drawing blood, but she scarcely noticed. *Have to get away*. The words chanted through her mind.

Walter was right behind her. She didn't spare the moment it would take to glance over her shoulder. She heard the pounding of his footsteps, the heaviness of his breathing as he quickly made short shrift of her head start.

She heard the whiz of an arrow as it sailed past. It

missed her by several feet and landed in a tree trunk up ahead of her. She knew better than to believe that he was such a poor shot. He was playing with her, taunting her with the knowledge that this was only the beginning.

As though to confirm that, he called out, "The next one will be closer. And the one after that closer still. We don't want the game to end too early, now do we? No fun in that."

Olivia recalled Walter's delight in hunting as a boy. Not for food, but for entertainment. The idea of killing animals for sport had repulsed her then. Now his fascination with hunting could very well end her life.

She didn't waste her breath in responding. She was too busy trying to keep ahead of him. Her lungs felt close to bursting, her calf muscles on fire as she pushed herself. Why hadn't she kept up her early morning jog?

Up ahead. A hollowed-out log. It was her only chance, if she could make it there without Walter seeing what she was doing. A burst of speed later, she reached it and slithered inside. She forced her breathing to quiet, her heartbeat to slow. Her body relaxed, the adrenaline ebbing as she focused on taking shallow breaths.

She heard him now. Coming to a stop. Looking around. Using a stick to poke at the thick underbrush.

A black beetle scurried over her arm. She stifled the scream that sprang to her lips. Silence was her only chance at survival. That and prayer.

Walter muttered something, stomped off. Or did he? She wouldn't put it past him to pretend to leave and then circle back. She didn't move. Couldn't. She waited five minutes. Ten.

Muscles cramped to the point of pain, she crawled out from the log and took a cautious look around. He was gone. At least for now. He could come back at any moment, but she was unharmed and could walk out of the marsh.

"Thank You, Lord." The words came automatically to her lips. He had never let her down. He never would.

Now to get out of here. The sun was rapidly sinking below the horizon, leaving only scant light as it filtered through the thick canopy of leaves.

It wasn't going to get any lighter. Or any easier.

She gauged the position of the lowering sun in the sky and got her bearings. She made a half-quarter turn. She put one foot in front of the other. Again.

What looked like a fallen branch suddenly moved. A snake. A cottonmouth by the look of it. A scream broke from her throat.

She clamped a hand over her mouth and looked around anxiously. If Walter were anywhere in the area, he'd surely have heard it. But there were no running footsteps, no sound at all except for those of the animals who made their homes in the marsh. She gave the snake a wide berth and kept moving.

All the while she prayed and drew courage from the faith that had sustained her for a lifetime.

Hurry. Hurry. The words pounded through Sal's mind with unrelenting persistence. He had to find Olivia before it was too late.

Timmons led the way. "I know this area like the back of my hand. My brother and I used to hunt here."

Sal nodded. A lot of wetlands had been hunted until there was nothing left. He'd never hunted, never wanted part of the ritual. The whole thing was rigged against the animals. He knew his attitude wasn't popular. Part of the coming of age for a boy in the South was the first hunt, bringing in a deer or, if he were fortunate, a bear.

He recognized the irony. He'd taken lives while serving his country…and maybe that was part of it. There was too much bloodshed in the world already.

If Jeppsen and Timmons had confided in him sooner, Sal could have prevented Olivia from getting as deeply involved as she had.

"Olivia's life is in danger because you didn't say anything. If Walter knows she's onto him, he's got no reason to keep her alive."

A deep flush crossed the agent's face. "I'm sorry about that. But I was under orders. I couldn't say anything. We have over two years in on this op. We couldn't blow it. The greater good and all."

The greater good. Sal had heard the phrase numerous times in his work. In his mind, the greater good was only an excuse and had little relationship to reality. "So you put an innocent woman in danger instead?" He understood national security, but this was Olivia's life they were talking about.

"You'd have done the same thing in my place," Timmons said, the color in his face deepening.

"I would never be in your place. I don't play with people's lives."

"We'll find your lady," Timmons promised.

"You'd better hope so. Because you'll be the first one I come for if we don't."

Olivia was running for her life. Twice, in less than a week, a man she'd thought of as a friend had tried to kill her.

"If I get out of this," she said to herself, "I've got to get a better class of friends."

Her humor fell flat. She was winded. Her flimsy sandals had given out miles earlier and her feet were shredded by the harsh terrain. Her skin was red and raw where mosquitoes the size of humming birds had feasted with greedy enthusiasm.

"Please, Lord," she prayed. "I'm scared. Sal doesn't

know where I am. It's You and me." The Lord was always with her.

She assessed her situation. She was hungry, cold and out of breath. She had no weapons. No, that wasn't right. She had her mind.

It was time she put it to work.

She either needed to keep moving or find some sort of hiding place. Was it only a few days ago that she and Sal had taken shelter in a cave?

So much had happened in the days following. Part of her was still reeling from the knowledge that both Calvin and Walter were working with terrorists, and once again she asked herself why she hadn't seen it. Because she hadn't wanted to?

There'd be time enough to sort it all out when she got out of the marsh. Not looking where she was going, she slipped in a rut and slid a dozen feet down a small incline. She berated herself for her carelessness, stood, and climbed back to the path.

Her whole body throbbed with exhaustion. She wanted nothing so much as to curl up and go to sleep. Shoulders set, she started off again, praying she was going in the right direction.

TWENTY-THREE

Sal and Timmons followed Walter and Olivia's tracks, all the while keeping an eye out for whoever was following them. Obviously, Walter didn't expect anyone to be tailing him because he'd made no attempt to obscure the trampled brush and grass. "How did the Chantrys come to be involved with Russian terrorists?"

"Junior served in the Middle East. As far as we can tell, he came home from the service with a list of black market contacts and put them to good use. One of those contacts had connections with an ex-Soviet scientist."

Another nod on Sal's part.

"Junior learned about a shipment of HEU and made sure it would be diverted. He and his old man took possession of it and secured it somewhere, somewhere we don't know about. That's what this whole thing has been about, locating the HEU and getting it out of circulation along with stopping the plans from getting into the wrong hands. Calvin Chantry decided to cut the Russians out of the deal and sell the plans and the HEU to the highest bidder.

"If they'd pulled it off, the old man and his kid stood to make a bundle. They'd be living the good life while I slog along trying to make it on a civil servant's salary."

"Why do you keep doing it?" Sal asked.

"Because I believe in the work." Passion rang through

the agent's voice. "My kids may never go to an Ivy League college, but I'm doing my best to make sure there's still a world for them to grow up in. If this HEU and the attack plans get to our enemies, part of that world is going to go up in radioactive ashes."

Sal's respect for the man grew. He had his head on straight and his priorities in place. "You're all right, Timmons."

The agent gave a mock salute. "Right back at you. I knew you were the real deal when we first met. I wish I could have told you what was going on. In retrospect, I probably should have. But orders are orders."

Sal understood, even respected it. As a soldier, he'd had to obey orders, some he hadn't always agreed with, some he'd spoken out against. But, because he had taken an oath to protect his country at all costs, in the end, he'd done what he'd been told.

"None of this helps us find your lady, though." Timmons lifted a hand to shield his eyes and scanned the unforgiving landscape of the marsh. "Even experienced hunters get lost in this."

Sal thought it through. Olivia was smart. If she'd managed to escape from Chantry, she'd head for high ground. There wasn't much high ground in the swamp, but the land elevated slightly toward the west.

It was all he had, so he headed in that direction, praying that he was right.

Olivia's steps dragged. She had tried to reach higher ground to get her bearings. Just when she thought she couldn't take another step, she heard it.

"Olivia."

Sal's voice. She turned to it. "Here! I'm here."

"Stay where you are. We'll come to you."

"Walter's out there. He has a crossbow."

"Stay put. We'll be there in a minute."

We? Who was with him?

True to his word, Sal burst through the underbrush a minute later. He pulled her to him.

She held on. "You found me."

"I'll always find you. The only thing that matters now is that we get you out of here and to a hospital to be checked out."

"No." The strength of her voice startled her. "No. We need to find Walter, stop him."

Agent Timmons stepped forward. "You know him best, Ms. Hammond. Will he keep coming after you or will he run?"

"Walter wants the money he and Calvin got from the Russians more than he wants to kill me. My guess is that he'll cut and run. He has a boat at the marina. I don't remember the name."

Timmons pulled up the marina's website on his phone. "Here's the list of boats registered. If you saw the name, would you recognize it?"

The three of them scanned the list.

Sal seized upon one. "The *Easy Day*. The SEAL motto is 'The only easy day was yesterday.' That's got to be it."

Olivia grabbed his hand. "We have to stop him. Before he sells what he knows."

He brushed her hair back from her forehead. "Do you know how beautiful you are? Beautiful and remarkable?"

"You're telling me this now? Now, when I'm covered with mud and muck and we have a terrorist to take down?"

"I had to."

Her heart turned over in her chest. "Tell me later. After we've stopped Walter."

"That's a promise."

Timmons worked the phone, filling in Homeland on where they were going. "Cavalry's coming."

They hiked back to where Sal and Timmons had left Jeppsen. "Stay with him," Sal said to Timmons. "I'm going for Walter."

Timmons started to object, then quieted when Sal shot him a hard look.

"You owe me."

"I guess we do at that."

Olivia laid a hand on Sal's arm, stopping him. "Not without me."

He shook his head. "Walter's desperate. Look at what he tried to do to you."

"I have to do this." She wasn't giving in. Not on this. She'd been held at knifepoint, shot at, tied up under a pier and drugged. She had to see this through to the end.

Another hike to Sal's truck took precious minutes. Sal disregarded every known traffic law and pulled up to the slip where the *Easy Day* was moored.

"There he is," Olivia cried.

Sal made it to the bow of the boat in three long jumps.

Sal and Walter squared off. Walter fought like the seasoned warrior he was. He knew every trick in the book. And then some.

He came at Sal, face twisted in a nasty grin.

Sal feinted to the left, drew his opponent's attention, then came in low, kicking out with his leg. His foot struck its mark and hit Walter in the thigh. Such a blow could temporarily cripple a man, but Walter wasn't stopped.

"Not bad, Santonni." He bared his teeth in a feral grin and drew a knife.

Sal didn't waste his breath talking. He needed every advantage he could get if he were to take Walter down.

"What's the matter, hero? Can't talk and fight at the same time?" Walter continued the same vein of trash talk.

Sal ignored it and focused on the goal. He didn't give an inch, and neither did Walter. They fought with arms and legs, fists and feet. Bending his body backward, Sal used Walter's own weight as he came at him, taking him to the ground, the knife clattering harmlessly to the deck.

Knee against his spine, hands clamped behind his back, Sal hunkered over the man who had tried to kill Olivia. Fury whipped through him, sent his blood to boil, his hands itching to wring the life from this piece of scum.

We're not like him. Olivia's words from under the pier where Calvin had held her captive filled Sal's mind, and he felt the worst of the rage dissolve. He pulled Walter to a kneeling position and looked for something with which he could bind the man's hands.

A muffled pop sounded.

TWENTY-FOUR

Olivia watched the tableau play out, saw the neat hole appear in Walter's chest. As the life flickered out of him and the acknowledgment that he was about to die appeared in his eyes, she thought she saw a whisper of the boy she had once known.

Sal grabbed her arm, pushed her down behind him. "The Russians," he mouthed.

Sal and Olivia crawled behind the wall of the boat's cabin. "Get out of here," he said. "I'll cover you. You can slip over the side."

"No way, soldier."

Two men boarded the boat. Sal took out the first one with a single shot but was a few moments too late to take the second. The man fired, his aim true, and Sal fell, a bullet to the chest. Olivia bent over him to shield him from further harm but was yanked up and away.

"Ms. Hammond, we meet again." The voice was rough and crude, holding a kind of cruel animal menace that caused gooseflesh to pepper her arms.

The voice from that first night. "It was you." Memories of that night, the threatening words, the hateful knife at her throat returned with a vengeance. The man had a white slab of a face, flat cheekbones framing a broad nose, and she recognized him as one of the men who had tried to force her into the van outside the courthouse. But it was the voice that had stuck in her mind.

"Yes. I have come for what is mine."

With a strength born of desperation to help Sal, she pulled away from her tormentor. She tore the tail from her shirt, stanched the blood that spurted from Sal's chest with terrifying force.

"Leave him. He is as good as dead." The callousness of the words sickened her. The man jerked her to her feet once more.

"You didn't have to kill Walter."

"He took what is mine. The uranium will cause much destruction, take many lives."

"You're a pig."

"And you will be dead. Along with your friend. You have interfered from the beginning. I should have killed you that night."

Olivia understood that he would make good on his words unless she did something now. "I have the drive with the information on it. I'll give it to you if you promise not to kill us." She whimpered, playing the part of the helpless woman to the hilt, and saw that the Russian had relaxed his posture. "I have to reach inside my pocket for it." As she pretended to do so, she struck out with her foot, catching him in the chest.

Shock that would have been comical at any other time crossed his face as he staggered, nearly falling. He heaved to a crouch, then propelled himself forward. He would have rammed into her, but, at the last moment, Olivia danced aside, pivoted and slammed the palm of her hand under his nose.

Blood gushed forth, and the Russian swiped at it with the back of his hand. A string of words exploded from his mouth.

Pain sang up her arm, but she hardly noticed it. She

was too busy fighting for her life. Hers and Sal's. She dropped to the ground, scythed her legs and knocked his feet out from under him. He crumpled to the deck. Before she could get to her feet, he snagged her ankle, pulled her down to him.

They wrestled there on the deck of the boat. He outweighed her by at least eighty pounds. She fought with everything she had, writhing and tossing from side to side, but it wasn't enough.

Hands, unbelievably strong, clamped around her neck, squeezed.

Deprived of oxygen, she grew weaker by the moment. She kicked, bucked, brought her fingers to his eyes to gouge them, but she was rapidly losing the battle. Her vision turned red, a mist she recognized as the beginning of the end.

Have to get up. Have to help Sal.

The words chanted through her brain. She thought she might have said them aloud. Triumph turned her opponent's eyes into slits. "Today you will die."

The words, delivered in a heavy accent, penetrated the fog of her brain. She drew on the last of her reserves.

There. The knife just out of reach. She stretched, strained until her fingertips touched it. Another quarter of an inch. The Russian didn't notice as he was too busy choking the life from her.

Dear Lord, help me. Her hand closed over the hilt of the knife, and she plunged the blade into his belly. Surprise skidded across his features. The hands around her neck loosened, and she gulped in a lungful of sweet air.

"No," she said, voice a hoarse rasp in her seared throat. "Today you die." With one last burst of strength, she pushed the man off her and crawled to where Sal lay, bleeding and broken.

"Livvie."

"Shh." She tore the other sleeve from her shirt and replaced the makeshift bandage of the first one, praying all the while. "Help's on the way."

Minutes, though it seemed like hours, later, police, EMTs and federal agents, led by Timmons, swarmed around them.

She was propped against the side of the cabin. Gentle hands ran over her.

"Sal." Her throat was raw, and it hurt to talk. She wet her lips, tried again. "Help Sal."

"He's being seen to." A young woman in a blue uniform took Olivia's vitals. "Right now, I need to see to you. Your throat feels like it's on fire, right?"

Olivia was given oxygen, her scrapes and scratches attended to, pain medication administered. She scarcely noticed as she looked about for Sal.

"Your friend's on his way to the hospital." The EMT sent her a kind look. "Where you belong as well."

Olivia went to the hospital but refused to be admitted. She found the front desk and explained that she was looking for news about Salvatore Santonni. The receptionist shook her head. "I'm sorry. I couldn't give out any information even if I had it, which I don't."

Sick with worry, Olivia turned away.

A voice boomed through the hallways. "Our son. Salvatore Santonni. He is here. We must see him. Now." A large man, dark hair liberally streaked with white, was being soothed by a tiny woman.

Sal's parents?

A nurse hurried to them. "Sir, ma'am, I'll take you to the doctor who will be operating on your son."

Olivia followed at a discreet distance until the nurse saw her and frowned. "Are you family?"

"No. I'm…a friend."

"I'm sorry, but you can't go any farther."

Fortunately, Nicco Santonni showed up at that moment. "She's as good as family," he said and introduced Olivia to his parents.

"You will come with us," Sal's mother said in a quiet but firm voice.

The nurse lifted her hands. "If it's okay with the family, then I guess it's all right."

The doctor, a slender woman in blue scrubs, appeared a few moments later. "I won't lie to you. Your son's condition is serious." She gave a rundown of what the surgery would entail. "But he's young and strong. If he survives the surgery, he should make it. We'll keep you posted."

Knees rubbery, Olivia sank into a green vinyl chair. "Thank you, Mr. and Mrs. Santonni, for allowing me to be here."

"It's Matteo and Rosa," Sal's mother said. "You are special to Salvatore. Of course you should be here."

Olivia visited the restroom and groaned when she saw herself in the mirror. She washed her face and did her best to smooth her hair. The bloodstained clothes would have to wait. She wasn't leaving the hospital until she had news about Sal.

The next hours passed in a blur of bad coffee, murmured voices and worry. Nicco had gone home to get clean clothes for his parents. When the doctor reappeared, Olivia stood, tensed.

"Your son came through the surgery," the doctor said, addressing Sal's parents. "The bullet missed his heart by an inch. You can see him for a few minutes. Only two visitors at a time, please."

Matteo and Rosa Santonni went first. When they returned, Rosa gestured for Olivia to go.

Olivia knew how bad she looked, but she wouldn't allow feminine vanity to keep her from seeing Sal. She caught her breath at the sight of him hooked up to a dozen wires and tubes. His face, normally rich with color, was alarmingly pale. She reached out and touched his hand.

He didn't stir. She contented herself by simply looking her fill.

His eyes opened briefly. "Olivia. You're…you're all right?" The words came haltingly, and she knew he paid a high price to get them out.

"I'm fine. You're going to be all right." Tender mercies, she thought. It could have ended so differently. No need to tell him now that he'd been in surgery for five hours. Nor was there any need to tell him that the doctor had said the bullet had missed his heart by an inch.

Sal closed his eyes. "Need to tell you…"

"It can wait."

His eyes opened briefly. "No. Can't wait."

A male nurse appeared, motioned that it was time for her to leave.

Olivia touched her fingertips to Sal's lips. As she walked back to the waiting room, she said a silent prayer of gratitude. Sal was going to be all right. It would take time for him to recover, but that was all right, too.

They both needed time.

One week. Seven days. One hundred and sixty-eight hours. Far too long to spend in the hospital for one measly bullet wound.

Sal tried to sit up on his own and lay back with a groan.

"You are impatient. Always." Rosa Santonni fussed over her older son. "Did you not hear the doctor? He said you must rest."

He struggled for the patience his mama told him he lacked. At the same time, he chafed at the knowledge that he couldn't will his body to heal faster.

Something good had come out of it, though. Haltingly, he'd told his parents about his time as the Hawk.

"Do you think we love you less?" his mama had demanded, tears gathering in her eyes. "We will never be anything but proud of you, our Salvatore."

"You served your country well. You are a hero," his father added.

Olivia had said much the same thing as they'd hidden in the cave. Thoughts of her prompted him to push his body into a sitting position, despite his mama's protests. He needed to tell Olivia something, and he couldn't do it while he was lying flat on his back. He learned she'd been there every day to see him but always when he was asleep. Had she purposefully timed her visits?

Over the last couple of years, he'd watched his friends fall in love. The path hadn't been smooth for any of them, but they'd persevered and found the proverbial pot of gold at the end of the journey in the form of a forever love.

Sal wanted that for himself. He wanted the happily-ever-after his parents and sisters and friends had found. He wanted the whole thing. He'd realized something else as well: the faith he'd thought he'd lost forever had returned there in the marsh as he'd prayed to the Lord to protect Olivia.

His parents, sisters and Nicco had visited, along with a parade of friends, including Shelley and Caleb Judd and Jake and Dani Rabb. Shelley told him that Homeland had found the HEU on Walter's boat and had put an end to the terrorists' plans.

Even Timmons and Jeppsen had stopped by, Jeppsen with his arm in a sling.

"The Russian survived and is singing his heart out," Timmons said. "Turns out he prefers to spend the rest of his life in a prison cell here in the good 'ol US of A rather than facing his terrorist buddies back in Russia."

"You came through for us, Santonni," Jeppsen added. "Thanks."

At any other time, Sal would have been gratified with the news. Right now, all he could think of was Olivia.

When his mama fussed with his pillow, he almost growled at her. "I need to see Olivia. I have to talk with her."

"You will see her when it is right. Now you must rest."

Olivia had been to the hospital every day, making certain that her visits coincided with Sal's sleeping schedule. She'd talked with his parents, brother and sisters, but she had yet to talk with Sal since the day of his surgery. She doubted he even remembered what they'd said.

So, okay, she was a coward.

She knew her heart, but she didn't know his. He'd rejected her love but had still come after her when Walter had taken her. He hadn't given up his need to protect her, which meant he still cared. Didn't it?

It was time to act like the responsible adult she was and face him. If he told her once again that there was nothing for them, she'd accept that and move on. Her heart would break all over again, but she'd deal with it.

In between trips to the hospital, she'd paid a visit to Bryan at jail, found him subdued but grateful that he'd been cleared of the kidnapping and murder charges.

"Thanks for doing what you did," he said, surprising her. "You didn't have to."

She prayed that Bryan would get the help he needed for his problems and maybe even make something of his life when he had served his time.

The partners at Chantry & Hammond had pooled their resources and decided to keep the firm going. As it was deemed unseemly to keep the name *Chantry* in the title, a debate was even now being waged as to which partner's name should go first in the firm's new letterhead. It didn't matter to Olivia. She planned to strike out on her own and do the kind of work her father had started out to do.

One week after Sal's surgery, she shored up her courage and made the now familiar trip to the hospital. Voice deliberately bright, she filled the room with chatter, not giving him the opportunity to speak.

"Sal. You're looking better. That's good. Really good. We won the court case. The parents will get a settlement. It won't be enough—how could it be? But we set a precedent for other such cases."

Sal waited until she paused for a breath. "I never doubted you."

"Your family is wonderful. I've gotten to know them—"

He held up a hand, cutting her off. "Thank you for saving my life."

"We saved each other."

"There's more. That night in the cave, you made me look at myself and what I did and why I did it." He shoved his hand through his hair. "I'll never regret serving my country. That's truth. I'm a different man than I was then. That's also truth."

"Truth matters. And here's another: you would never be anything other than honorable."

"That's what my parents said. I told them about my role as the Hawk. You were right about them."

"I'm glad. For you and for them." She let her gaze move over him, felt the familiar lift and squeeze of her heart.

He took her hand in his. "I was running scared from my faith. It turned out I'd never stopped believing, I'd just forgotten how." The breath he drew was shaky. "That's not the only thing I was running from. I was afraid to admit that I loved you. You are everything I want, everything I need. You make me more than I am."

Unbearably touched, she looked at this man who had

found his way into her heart and knew that she would love him forever.

"I want it all," he said, voice hoarse. "A wife. A family. A dog who drools. Bicycles in the driveway. Skateboards on the porch."

"You can have it," she said softly. "All you have to do is reach for it."

"Are...are you sure?"

"I know what's here." She flattened her hand over his heart.

"I love you."

She leaned closer so that she could brush her lips over his. "That's all I need, all we need. We have each other and the Lord. Nothing else matters."

"You are everything to me," he said and managed to return the kiss, despite the wires and tubes.

Life wasn't perfect, but sometimes there were moments that were perfect enough.

* * * * *

*If you enjoyed SHATTERED SECRETS,
look for these other great books from author
Jane M. Choate, available now.*

KEEPING WATCH
THE LITTLEST WITNESS

Find more great reads at www.LoveInspired.com

Dear Reader,

I hope you have enjoyed Sal and Olivia's story.

When I started this series several years ago, I wasn't certain I could tell Sal's story as he wanted it told. He is a strong man with a gentle side, as the best men are. But I didn't understand him until I realized that he was struggling to forgive himself. And then I knew I could write about him, because I struggle to forgive myself as well. Olivia helped Sal remember that the Lord is always on his side, always ready to forgive him.

Sal and Olivia didn't have an easy time of it. Their love path was punctuated with embezzlers and killers. Most of us won't have to deal with that kind of conflict, but we, like Olivia and Sal, have to work at keeping our love alive and strong. With the Lord's help, we can find our own happy endings.

With love in the Lord,
Jane

Get 2 Free Books,
Plus 2 Free Gifts—
just for trying the Reader Service!

LIS17R

Katerina Garwood was halfway between one of the stables
and the house, heading for her old suite, when she saw an
imposing black vehicle pass beneath the ornate wrought
iron arch at the foot of the drive. Unexpected company was
all she needed. If her father came outside to see who it was
and caught her trespassing on his precious property he'd be
furious. Well, so be it. There was no way she could run and
hide in time to avoid encountering the new arrival—and
perhaps her irate dad, as well.

Chin high, she paused in the wide, hard-packed drive
and shaded her eyes. The SUV reminded her of one that
had assisted the county sheriff on the worst day of her
life. The day when all her dreams of a happy future had
vanished like a puff of smoke.

Dark-tinted windows kept her from getting a good look
at the driver until he stopped, opened his door and stepped
partway out. Prepared to tell him to go to the house if he
needed to speak to someone in charge, she took one look
and was momentarily speechless. The blond, blue-eyed

man was so imposing and had such a powerful presence he sent her usually normal reactions whirling. When he spoke, his deep voice magnified those unsettling feelings.

"Katerina Garwood?"

"Do I know you?"

"No, but I know you. I'm Special Agent West. I'd like to talk to you about Vern Kowalski."

"I have nothing to say." She started to turn away.

"This is not a social call, Ms. Garwood." He flashed a badge and blocked her path. "I suggest you reconsider."

"FBI? You have to be kidding. I am so normal, so boring, that until recently people hardly noticed me."

"They do now, I take it."

She blushed and rolled her eyes. "Oh, yeah."

"Then you'll understand why I need to speak with you."

Don't miss
SPECIAL AGENT by Valerie Hansen,
available wherever
Love Inspired® Suspense ebooks are sold.

www.LoveInspired.com

*Will a pretend courtship fend off matchmaking mothers,
or will it lead to true love?*

Read on for a sneak preview of
THEIR PRETEND AMISH COURTSHIP,
the next book in **Patricia Davids**'s
heartwarming series, **AMISH BACHELORS**.

"Noah, where are you? I need to speak to you."

Working near the back of his father's barn, Noah
Bowman dropped the hoof of his buggy horse Willy, took
the last nail out of his mouth and stood upright to stare
over his horse's back. Fannie Erb, his neighbor's youngest
daughter, came hurrying down the wide center aisle,
checking each stall as she passed. Her white *kapp* hung
off the back of her head dangling by a single bobby pin.
Her curly red hair was still in a bun, but it was windblown
and lopsided. No doubt, it would be completely undone
before she got home. Fannie was always in a rush.

"What's up, *karotte oben*?" He picked up his horse's
hoof again, positioned it between his knees and drove in
the last nail of the new shoe.

Fannie stopped outside the stall gate and fisted her
hands on her hips. "You know I hate being called a carrot
top."

"Sorry." Noah grinned.

He wasn't sorry a bit. He liked the way her unusual violet eyes darkened and flashed when she was annoyed. Annoying Fannie had been one of his favorite pastimes when they were schoolchildren.

Framed as she was in a rectangle of light cast by the early-morning sun shining through the open top of a Dutch door, dust motes danced around Fannie's head like fireflies drawn to the fire in her hair. The summer sun had expanded the freckles on her upturned nose and given her skin a healthy glow, but Fannie didn't tan the way most women did. Her skin always looked cool and creamy. As usual, she was wearing blue jeans and riding boots under her plain green dress and black apron.

"What you need, Fannie? Did your hot temper spark a fire and you want me to put it out?" He chuckled at his own wit. He along with his four brothers were volunteer members of the local fire department.

"This isn't a joke, Noah. I need to get engaged, and quickly. Will you help me?"

Don't miss
THEIR PRETEND AMISH COURTSHIP
by Patricia Davids, available June 2017 wherever
Love Inspired® books and ebooks are sold.

www.LoveInspired.com

LIEXP0517